This book holds 'a baker's dozen' worth of laughter, love, life; prepared, cooked, seasoned and served with care. The stories are served individually, and as a whole, in the hope they will stimulate the reader's spirit in the same way an experience of eating fish and chips by the beach can nourish a person's body and soul.

'Suzanne Robinson Pollard brings understanding and wisdom into everyday life as you read her books. I have been truly blessed by these 'parables for today'. It is easy to let some things in our day just slip past without seeing their part in the bigger picture. Well done, Suzanne. Thank you, I have enjoyed reading every story.' — Elaine Hans

'I struggled with reading for a long time, but I find Suzanne's stories hold my attention and are easy to read. The stories are interesting, enlightening, positive, encouraging and very inspiring. I really enjoy them and find that they are a real blessing. My favourite is the rain drops.' —Lynelle Wallace

'Suzanne's gift to write brings inanimate objects to life, and her insightful knowledge of the relevant subject brings to the reader a greater understanding, and appreciation, for the particular truth the story is imparting.' —Suzette Baker

A Baker's Dozen

Laughter, Love, Life

Contemporary Short Stories for Today's Reader

Encouraging Reflective, Nourishing

Fish and Chips for the Spirit

Suzanne Robinson Pollard

Published by Suzzane Pollard 2015

Copyright © 2002 Suzanne Robinson Pollard

Book cover design and formatting services by BookCoverCafe.com

www.suzannerobinsonpollard.com.au
T/A Exemplar Parables for Today

First Edition 2015

ISBN:
978-0-9925823-2-6 (pbk)
978-0-9925823-3-3 (ebk)

*To my family and friends, for your patience
when I was passionate, thank you.
To people who have shared with me how
these stories are now a source of personal
encouragement to you, thank you.
For the gift to write, and the courage to put
pen to paper, I give all the honour to God.*

Contents

Preface

This book is a compilation of parables for today's world, a baker's dozen—thirteen stories of hope. People have asked me why thirteen?

I thought at first it was like a baker charging for twelve buns but packing an extra one as a gift to the buyer. Slowly, over time, I realised that Jesus and His disciples were the baker's dozen. What they did was to spread healing, forgiveness and acceptance to everyone willing to allow the words of God's love to fill their hearts.

Another question I have been asked is where did the stories come from?

I have been blessed to be able to see things around me as having individual personalities. Through this ability I am able to imagine that everything, and everyone, has a story to tell. I would often find myself writing stories in my head, scribbling notes on bits and pieces of scrap paper.

It was only when my children left home and I was no longer doing the thing I loved most—being a hands-on mother—that I thought to ask myself what I enjoyed doing.

The answers I got were interesting, to say the least.

I love to sit in the shade by water, or in a park and see the beauty in God's creation. I like to sit in open-air cafes, to consider the traffic and the people as they hurry on their way within their own busy worlds. I love to sit quietly and contemplate the many places in the world where I would like to take a moment to enjoy a cup of coffee. I love to relax, close my eyes and listen to the sounds in the environment around me.

I love to tell stories and I am known for starting conversations with 'once upon a time in the land of nod …' (this particular trait drives my friends crazy).

I love to encourage people to see their life bucket is half full rather than half empty.

It was however, only when I began to write words to encourage did I realise how much I truly enjoyed putting my thoughts onto paper for others to read.

So, these stories are a few that have built in my heart and my head, until they broke free to be scribbled down onto the back of an envelope. Sometimes I would be racing for the computer still dripping wet from a shower at 11:00 o'clock at night. Usually when driving some distance, I stop only long enough to refresh myself and fill up the petrol tank, but once, while I was driving to visit my newly born grandson, I stopped for a two-hour lunch break to begin a story. Often I have woken before the dawn thinking, *I'll just make a note of those new ideas, it should only take a few minutes*, only to discover, with surprise, I had not only missed breakfast but was close to missing lunch as well.

My journey of discovery, through the personalities of my characters, has been wonderful and enlightening. To be able to share with my readers the knowledge that God is faithfully, lovingly, waiting to be invited into every situation is a very great honour that I take seriously.

When writing these stories, I found myself frowning, laughing and crying as the characters and the stories came to life. I hope you, when reading these stories, will be touched by the reality of my characters and their situation. My hope is that these stories will touch something in the hearts of those who read them. I believe that even though every story is for everyone, the stories are like the times and the seasons in our lives. One story, at different times, will have more relevance to the reader's current situation and circumstances than at other times.

Just a Little Wooden Box

For Gemma

He could feel the vibrations of the men packing everything around him. They were moving house—yet again! It really was none of his business, because his opinion would not alter what was happening around him, but he could not help wondering *where they were going this time.*

The last time they had moved, laughter had rolled all around him and filled the other moving crates in the room. Last time the large moving crate he was in moved around a lot. It had been lifted up, dropped with a thump, and then creaked as it rubbed against the crates beside it. He had been very glad he had been encased in a cloud of bubble wrap; otherwise, he was sure he would have been damaged. The last time, he had not held his treasure inside of him.

Unlike the other items around him, who often boasted they had been specially purchased to live

13

in this room, or that room, he knew he had been purchased because he easily fitted into all the rooms. He had special places in all the rooms of the house. This could have been a problem with the others living in the different rooms, but he had been made in love, and knew his worth, so he did not need to boast of all the rooms he lived in.

He knew he was different, that he had been made for a different purpose: he had been made to live in humility. He was beautiful in his own way, but those who placed value on big, or shiny, or glitzy easily overlooked his understated, excellent craftsmanship. He was just a little box—and today he was being packed in the top of a big moving crate.

He remembered his time in bubble wrap as a feeling of bouncy comfort. But today he had been placed inside a cardboard box, wrapped in shredded paper to keep him warm and dry. His people had wrapped big straps of sticky tape around and around the shredded paper. He knew this because each time he heard the 'screech' of the tape as it was pulled off its roll, the paper around him became tighter and tighter. His little key, which was normally secured under his bottom piece, had been placed in its lock, and then half turned to stop it from falling out.

He was only a little box, about the size of two matchboxes. He could so easily have been left behind. The love he had been made with gave him peace about that, because his people had written on the outside of the cardboard box: 'Important—pack last.' He knew this meant he would be unpacked first, at the end of their journey. He had heard the room emptying around. He knew this, because he could hear the hollowness of the people's footsteps as they moved around the room. His was to be the last crate into the moving van, and he knew this too because he had heard his people say, 'Put all the other crates on first but this one,' and he had felt his person's hand rest on the outside of his crate. 'This one goes on last.'

He had been with 'his people' now for nearly ten years. How did he know this? He had heard 'his people' say, when they packed him away this time, 'So, little box, it will be ten years next month since you came to us.' Then he had been cradled in his people's hands for long minutes before being wrapped in the shredded paper. His people's voice had been a little muffled, but still he heard. 'How wonderful it has been to see you so happily received.' Knowing how carefully they tended to him, he looked forward to spending many more years with his people.

Whether this 'nearly ten years' was his actual years or not, he did not care. Once, he had been sitting next to a glass jar which had boasted she was over eighty years old. She had constantly talked of how her lovely green colour was very valuable, and how other people, over the years, had wanted to own her. The little wooden box could not comprehend her fascination with the passing years. He had only really 'existed' since the time his people had found him on a dusty middle shelf in a small general store. He had only begun to live when the love his maker had put into him was touched by the warmth, and love, his people had for each other.

He had been made with care, using several different types of wood. His corners met with precision, with inter-connecting shapes. He was glued, pegged and lacquered, and there were no gaps to let in the damp air. He knew he was strong because although his little pieces of wood were tiny, the pattern they made strengthened each small piece. He had been given a small lock. It was so small the maker had to order it especially for him. His little lock was gold in colour and highlighted the wood used in his pattern. His lid overlapped his sides by a third of their width. And in the overlap, in the middle of his height, his golden lock had been placed in the middle of his belly.

He had waited patiently on the shelf in the store, and even though dust had gathered around him, and also settled on top of him, it had not touched him. He knew this because when his people had picked him up and blown gently onto him, the dust had taken flight. It had softly drifted away to settle on the other items for sale, with whom he shared his corner. With his coat of dust gone, his lock, and key had gleamed in a ray of sunlight as it slipped through the dusty window and touched him.

He never knew what he held inside himself. He did not know why his people regarded it as so important that it needed to be locked away. He had often felt it, touched it with the warmth that was his insides. It was only because he had seen and heard how the different things around him moved and sounded that he knew what he held was made of paper. He had felt around it, and found that the paper had corners, just like his. What he did not know was that, at first, the paper had been way too big to fit inside him. So it had been folded over and over, until it was small enough to rest inside him.

Still his people, or rather one of them, would often pick him up and hold him close. So close that the little box could hear his people's heartbeat then he heard them sing his people; sing a little melody that he did not understand. Then, very carefully, he would be placed carefully on a shelf, and his people would go about their day. If he ever took time to think about it, he would realise that 'his people' had only been 'one person' for a long time. But if he were ever asked, the little box would have to said, 'I do not know when "two" became "one". It is not my job to know these things. I just am, and I am made to be the best I can be, by being me.

I am made to keep safe what I am given, and to give happiness to those in the world around me.'

And he had done just that; he had been the best little box with a lock that he could be. Because he was true to what he was made to do, he had been found by people who made sure that he was kept warm and safe. He still did not know why he was important, but he was happy to be so because it meant that his people ensured he was packed each time they moved.

And so now, today, they were moving again.

Unknown to the driver of the van, a rain storm had swept through the valley during the night, and the integrity of road surface had disintegrated into holes and had become dangerous. The van driver, in his efforts to avoid them, began to swerve all over the road. The moving van lurched, and lunged, in the uneven surface of the road. The little box became used to the creaking and the groaning of the crates around him as they shifted together, riding the van's uneven rhythm as best they could.

Without warning, the uneasy rhythm of the crates in the back of the van was rudely interrupted by an ear-splitting, resounding 'bang', and his world became a tumbling mess. The van's tailgate dropped, and the back door swung open, exposing the moving crates to the weather. The van lurched again, spitting several crates out onto the road. The crates landed hard and tumbled end over end. The tape sealing the crates shut broke, and contents of the bruised crates were scattered over the wet, holey road. One of the ejected, open crates had contained the little wooden box.

Suddenly, and unexpectedly, the little box's world had changed. One moment he had been warmly dozing, the next he was being tossed around, and thrown out of the safety of his big crate into a damp, uncertain night. As the lid of the crate fell off, his cardboard box broke into two pieces, and out flew the taped-up ball of shredded paper. Over and over it rolled, as it fell onto the muddy verge of the road and down a steep riverbank. The wet grass on the bank reached out, with soggy hands, and tried to slow down the ball of paper, but the wet hands and the sticky tape made the ball impossible to catch. Shaken and disorientated, the little box was glad when he came to a sudden stop within the roots of a big, old tree.

The little box did not know where he was, but he thought that he might be near water. This thought was confirmed when he began to feel moisture creeping up into his shredded-paper protection. He was suddenly afraid that it would reach into his insides, and damage his treasure. He did not worry that he might be lost. He did not worry that he might not be found. No, he knew that if he were lost, then he would be found.

Because he knew his people would look and look until they found him.

His worry was that when they found him, his hidden treasure would be damaged by the moisture seeping up through the shredded paper towards him. He knew he had been made, purposely, to be able to resist water. He decided there and then that he would trust his maker. He would keep his cool, hold onto his hinges, and keep his lid tightly closed. He decided to hold onto the promise given by his maker, that he would be water resistant.

The little wooden box knew that he could not remove himself from the danger of seeping water, but he chose to do what he was able to do. He would not panic; he would wait patiently, he would trust his maker's promise, and he would keep his treasure safe until his people found him. After making his decisions, the little box put them into action by hugging himself tight, and waiting.

The little box did not know that the van driver, when he had quickly repacked the open crates, had not seen him hidden within the roots of the tree. He did not know he had been left behind, so he sat in the middle of his shredded paper and waited to be found. Sometime later, when the rain had stopped, the little box's people came to search for him. He could feel they were near the tree, but because he was only a little wooden box with no voice, he could not call out and say,

'Here I am. Come and get me.' He could only sit tight, protect his hidden treasure, and wait until he was found.

So there he nestled, within the root system of the great old tree, on the side of the river. He waited, and listened to the sounds of people moving around him. He listened to dogs barking, at what he did not know. He heard the dogs splashing in water as they chased balls thrown to them by their people. He heard motorboats going up and down on the river. He felt the vibration of manmade waves lapping at the riverbank close to his resting place. At first he had been afraid that the boats would push the water higher, into his paper, but then he remembered he had been made for a purpose. And he trusted the water would not reach him, trusted nothing would happen to him, until he had returned his treasure to his people. So he waited, with peace in his heart, in the soddened, mangled mess that had once been freshly shredded paper. The paper had been put around him to protect him, and even in its state of disintegration its centre held fast around the little box, and kept away the outside elements.

He was not sure how long he waited, because he was, after all, only a little wooden box. He just kept on waiting, knowing deep in his heart that one day his people would come and find him.

How could they not? He held a precious treasure, something that his people wanted. Something they needed to touch and see every day of their lives.

One day, when the sun was shinning, people were calling to each other and boats were roaring around on the river. A small, shaggy dog shoved her nose deep into the roots of the old tree. After all the time he had spent watching the world along the riverbank, the little wooden box had been startled when a wet black nose had nudged at his wrapping. He could not stop the small dog from loosening what was left of the paper that had surrounded him. The little box did not know whether he was relieved, or apprehensive, when the small dog succeeded in pulling him free from his hiding place.

The small dog, however, was extremely pleased with herself; her tail wagged and wagged when she came out from amongst the tree roots with something in her mouth. The little wooden box, amid the mess being carried loosely in the small dog's mouth, heard a young lady call to her pet. The small dog trotted happily over to her person, pleased to be able to bring her the present she had found. She wagged her tail, dropped her mouthful of mess on the ground, and sat down to see how pleased her person would be with the gift.

The young lady reached into the rotting mess, and pulled out the little box covered in grunge and grime. The young lady saw what she thought might be a rusted little key held tight in its lock. After giving it a couple of little tugs and was not successful in dislodging the key, the young lady turned her efforts to rubbing some of the grime off the back of the little box. With only a couple of wipes with a tissue, she saw that its hinges, previously bright yellow, were intact but now speckled with black spots and dirt. The owner of the small dog nearly threw the little box away again, but just as she was about to drop it into a big blue bin smelling of old fish, and filled to the top with leftover food, something held her hand. After a moment, she pulled out a small plastic bag, which had previously held a sandwich for her lunch, and put the little box inside, then tucked it back into her knapsack, called her small dog, and went home.

Home, for this young lady, was a one-bedroom flat over her shop. She was a shopkeeper and her shop was on the main road of the tourist town, overlooking the river. Her shop sold souvenirs to the tourists, who came to enjoy the river and parklands alongside the highway. After washing and oiling the little wooden box so that it glowed clean, she placed it on the bottom shelf of her front display window.

The lady shopkeeper did not feel that she was to even put a price on the little box. Whether it was because her small dog had found it and she had not bought it for stock, or something else, she did not know. All she knew was, she had to clean it and place it in her window in the hope that, some day, someone might see it and ask after it. All through the cleaning process, the lady shopkeeper had been unable to turn the key in its lock. However, she did not try to pry the lid open because the lady shopkeeper had the strangest idea that only when the little box was ready would the key turn one day.

And she was right, because the little box did not recognise her touch; he would not let go of his tight grip on his little key. And so the lady shopkeeper looked after the little wooden box even though she did not know what it held so safely inside.

Several months went by. The little box sat on the shelf and waited. He did prefer the dry shop shelf and the warmth of the sun to lying in a sodden mess under the tree's roots. Each day he held his secret tight within himself and waited, expecting to be found by his people.

One day, a man was walking past the little shop when he stopped to browse at the colourful display the lady shopkeeper had designed in the window. The man was casually looking at each shelf in turn when he went very still. His breathing slowed, from the hope or maybe it was from the shock, of what he had glimpsed on the bottom shelf. He squatted down to sit on his heels so that he could look more closely at the bottom shelf. Puzzled, he leaned in close, frowned in concentration, rubbed his chin and wondered, *Could it be? After all this time, could it possibly be?*

The man straightened and, before he could think too much about coincidence or answered prayer, walked to the doorway of the shop. Pushing open a multi-coloured glass door, he did not even hear the soft jingle of its little bell as he entered the shop. Looking around to discover who was in charge of the shop, the man walked over to the person by the cash register. Before the lady shopkeeper could ask to help him, the man asked about the little wooden box he had seen in the window. She told him how her small dog had found it under a tree. 'When I saw it all covered in dirt and mud, I very nearly threw it away as rubbish. But something stayed my hand, right over the bins, and in the end I brought it home and cleaned it up.'

The lady shopkeeper shared with the man how she had spent many days carefully cleaning all the grime away. 'But it did not matter how much oil I put on it or, how hard I tried, I was unable to turn the key in the little box's lock. I was happy to clean it and to restore the outside beauty of the little box, but I cannot guarantee what the inside is like. I did not feel to put a price on it, because it was found and did not belong to me. I placed it on the bottom shelf because I felt it would only be found by someone who was really looking to find it.'

'Come,' she said, indicating with her hand the direction she was going. Carefully, because the room was filled with colourful stock to sell, the man followed the lady shopkeeper through her display tables. Expectation filled his heart and, for the first time in a long time, he felt like singing aloud the well-remembered tune filling his head. Once they had reached the front display window shelf, the lady shopkeeper lifted up the little box from his place on her bottom shelf and handed it to the man.

Suddenly, the little box was alive and excited. He felt the touch of his people! He could feel the love, the wonder coming from someone who knew the treasure he held deep within himself. If the little box could sing, his song of happiness would have filled the heavens; as it was, the whole of his little wooden frame glowed from the inside. He did not care that no one but his maker would ever know that he was able to glow with happiness; he knew and he glowed. He had known, in his heart, that if he waited patiently, if he held hope in his heart, his people would find him. He had had faith that they would never stop looking for him.

So, when he felt his people's touch, he let go. For the first time in a long time, he loosened his grip on the little key. When the man turned it, it moved, and released the lock. The little box did not see the lady shopkeeper lift her hand to her mouth, gasping in surprise at the key turning so easily. She reached out her hand, touching the man's arm to get his attention, and said, 'It can't be that easy. In all this time the little box has sat on my shelf I have never been able to turn the key.'

The man smiled at her. 'The difference is, I know this little box, and it knows me. We have memories together, and have made promises to each other to always believe in miracles.' He told the lady shopkeeper how he had been looking for many months, ever since his moving van had lost and damaged some of his boxes in the move. He told her how he used to hold the little box in his hand, and sing his songs to it. 'I know this must all sound a little odd to you, but it is true. I would sing because inside this little box is one of the most precious things in my life.'

He gently opened the lid of the little box, and lifted out a folded piece of paper. The paper was not old, but neither was it new. It looked as though it had been opened and refolded many times. But still the creases were clearly defined. The shopkeeper saw that although the little box had spent many months in the damp by the river's edge, the paper looked as dry and clean as the day it was placed inside the box. The man handed the tiny piece of paper to the shopkeeper for her to see. While looking at what was written on that scrap of paper, tears filled the lady shopkeeper's eyes. Inside the folded piece of paper was a child's drawing showing a man in flowing robes and long black hair, holding a little girl in his arms, and they were both smiling. Underneath, in crooked, ill-formed letters was a message, from the heart of a little girl who loved her daddy.

Daddy, I am going to live with Jesus for a while, where I will no longer be sick. Don't be very sad, Daddy, because Jesus tells me this is a happy place. I love you and I will miss you VERY much. But Jesus tells me we will be together again in Heaven, and that you should know He loves you very much.

With tears running down her cheeks, the lady shopkeeper handed back the precious letter. There were no words to say. A little girl, who now lived in Heaven, had said it all. The man gave the lady shopkeeper a *thank-you* hug, and took his little wooden box, with its treasure, home.

The little wooden box still did not know what it was he had kept so safe. He did not know why he had been trusted to carry this reminder of Jesus' love for his people. All he knew was he had been lost, away from the touch he remembered. But now he was found, and was being restored to the place where he would be treasured for the rest of time. He, a little wooden box, carved with love, purchased out of love, given in love, holding a message telling the greatness of God's love, was going home again.

Three Little Stars

Three little stars were shaken from a purple cellophane packet as a little girl ran down the ramp to the train station. Nicole was her name but her mummy called her Nicki. She was so excited; this was to be her first real train trip. Nicki lived in the city with her parents. She had travelled with her mum on the city trains, but she did not count them as 'real' train trips. No, today she was going on a 'real' train trip. This train was going out of the city, and into the country. Nicki was going to visit with her grandparents. The train would travel for almost two hours. Now that, to Nicki, was a 'real' train trip.

Nicki would be away from home for a very long time. A whole week! And she had worried about how her mum and dad would live without seeing her every day.

When she told them about her concerns, they had answered, 'We will do very well.' But Nicki knew they would not, so she had left behind her favourite teddy bear—her very, very pink, Pink Lady Bear—to watch over them.

When Nicki's friend Cindy came to visit, Nicki was packing for her holiday. Cindy said that she would miss Nicki very badly. Nicki had looked at Cindy, and said, 'I will miss you, too. I promise to think of you every day.'

Cindy, before she left to go home with her mother, gave Nicki a packet of little stars to take with her. The little stars were no bigger than one of the buttons on Nicki's coat. When Nicki opened the packet, she saw the little stars were made of a shiny material that sparkled. Nicki had immediately loved them, given her friend a big hug, and put the packet of stars into her backpack.

When her mum took her to the train station, Nicki was so excited she could not get the seatbelt open. Her mum came to help her and warned her that if she did not 'settle down' she would make herself sick. Nicki answered, 'Yes, Mummy.' But as soon as Nicki was out of the car and had her backpack on her shoulders, she began to run down the ramp, which went under the train tracks, to the station platform.

'Nicki! Slow down!' her mother called to her. 'Nicki, stop! Stop right now, right where you are!'

Nicki was already halfway down the ramp, but as soon as her mum called to her she obeyed her mum and stopped where she was. But instead of standing quietly, Nicki began to jump up and down, calling for her mum to hurry up. In her excitement, Nicki had forgotten that the open packet of little stars was tucked into the side pocket of her backpack. Without Nicki noticing, with every little jump the little stars were being tossed out of their packet, scattered around the ramp and blown onto the station platform.

One little star landed between two stones on a rock wall running alongside of the ramp. One little star fell into some grass that was growing in tufts along a cement gutter at the bottom of the rock wall. And one little star flew out, hit a steel column that was supporting the overhead train tracks, and fell, to be wedged behind a large, rough bolt at the foot of the column. Other little stars fell onto the ramp itself, and were quickly moved to and fro by the movement of feet. The feet belonged to busy people who had no time to see the pretty little sparkling stars; they were focused only on catching their trains.

One little boy smiled and pulled away from his mama when he saw the stars moving around the platform. He swapped the jelly snake he was sucking on to his left hand, and reached down to gather some shiny stars with his lolly-covered fingers. His smile turned to a frown when he discovered that the little stars, in his sticky hand, were not only stuck together but were now dull and dismal to look at. The little boy shook his hand to be rid of the gooey mess and ran back to his mama.

Two small, brown-speckled sparrows dashed for a little red star. Beak to beak, they looked at each other as they held tightly to opposing corners. In unison, the sparrows pulled backward, not only to win the prize for themselves, but to also tear it open. Neither one of them would let go because, surely, this tempting, soft-shelled pod should have something good to eat inside it. And if it did then it would be theirs. So intent on their mission were the little birds that they did not notice the presence of a large tabby cat. The cat, however, was not as interested in the little sparrows as it was in the strange things that were moving around his platform. So, ignoring the sparrows, he crouched low and crept up to bat at a little yellow star with his paw.

All day the little stars were moved around the train station by the speeding feet of busy people. By evening most of the pretty little glittering stars were gone. It was as though there had never been a carpet of stars on the ramp at all. Out of the whole packet, only three remained, but they had fallen elsewhere.

One day went by, then another, and another, and still the three little stars remained hidden from the people. The places they had fallen protected them from the sneaky little wind that blew up the ramp; so they lay undisturbed, hidden, waiting. Even the little stars did not know what they lay waiting for. The little stars stayed bright and shiny, but still they lay undetected, waiting and watching the people go by.

Then one day there was a stirring in the air. The little three stars, lying in out-of-the-way places, felt an inner excitement. A man, bowed in the leg and bent in the back, shuffled his way to the ramp. He was moving slowly, painfully, taking his time. He glanced at the display of items for sale in the windows of shops leading to the entrance of the ramp. He was in no hurry; he knew his destination, but had not set a time to arrive at it. Every now and then the old man would stop and look into the faces of the people rushing by him.

Men and women, both, hurried purposefully past him. He did not know what he was looking for, but whatever it was he hoped to see, it was not there. After each pause in his journey, the old man carefully, deliberately, returned to his shuffling pace. There was no need to hurry as he only had one appointment to keep, and it was of his own making. The old man had not bothered to bring his walking stick; he would not need it later. However, to feel a little less exposed and vulnerable, he kept close to the rock wall as he made his way down the ramp.

Suddenly, a ray of sunlight flashed on something caught in the grass that was growing through cracks in the cement gutter. This utilitarian piece of engineering, built to carry rainwater to the sewers below the city, could be found alongside almost every public wall in the city. It was so common it was usually passed unnoticed.

The old man, with his bent back and bowed legs, had time, however, and was curious about the flash of colour he had seen. He moved slowly to the tuft of grass, highlighted by the ray of sunlight. He hung onto the edge of the rock wall, and, not really expected to find anything of interest, kicked at the grass with his foot. Then, feeling every ache in his body, he bent down, parted the stalks of the tuft of grass, and gathered up into his hand the thing that shone so brightly for only a brief moment of time.

When he opened his hand, he peered at the scrape of red satin in the shape of a little heart that he held. Turning the little star over with his forefinger, the old man read the word 'Love', which was written in white on the little star. While looking at the little word, written so simply on such a tiny thing, his eyes misted over.

Love—that was something he used to have in his life.

His dear wife of fifty-eight years was gone. She had gone on without him. Gone ahead of him to Heaven and he was feeling lost; he could not find any hope for his future without her.

His name was Roger. He had never thought there would be a time without his beloved wife. He missed her dreadfully, and had been looking for, and praying for, a sign. Something anything to give him reason to live without her. But there had been nothing. In the long weeks since Stella's death, nothing had come to guide him. But now, here in his hand, was something so unexpected, he thought, *It has to be a message. Why else would it be here this day, at this time? A tiny red star with the word love on it. It has to be the sign I asked for.*

Her favourite colour had been red. Rose red. And he had always thought of his beautiful Stella as a star that shone in the darkness of life just for him. Only Stella and God knew he thought of her in that way.

Stella had come into his life so many years ago, when he had been struggling with living a 'normal' life after returning from the war. Her soft ways had healed Roger's wounded heart and mind. She had been his angel sent by God. And he could not remember a time without her.

Stella's love had shone for him. Even as this little star in his hand had shone in the sunlight, Stella had been as bright and constant as the evening star in his life. Looking at the little star, Roger heard her last words speak into his heart: 'Remember, love, as much as I love you, there is One who loves you more. And He will see you through. I am with you, I am always with you, and so is God.'

How could I have forgotten?

How could I have forgotten that her love would stay with me forever?

How could I have forgotten that she would always be with me in my heart?

Roger looked at the little red star and popped it into his pocket. It was such a little thing, a tangible something that he believed had come in his time of despair. It was a tangible something to remind him of his Stella, and her promise to him. The word on the little scrap of material said 'Love'; he believed it was a reminder that although Stella was no longer in her earthly body, she would always be with him, no matter where he was or what he was doing.

He closed his gnarled old fingers around the little star, and knew, as he placed it into his coat pocket, that he would carry the little star with him always. He would keep it in his pocket and reach for it when he missed her too much.

Holding it, and touching it, would remind him that love surrounded him. God's message of love, in the shape of a little star, would continue to give him the strength, and peace of heart, to survive until he too could travel the pathway to heaven, and be reunited with his Stella.

Roger turned to go back up the ramp and return to their home—his home. It was just two short blocks from the train station. His plan had seemed so simple this morning, when he had closed his front door and walked away from their home. He had tidied the rooms and then put on his best clothes. When he had left the house, he had made up his mind he would not return. He could no longer live alone in their house. He had decided it would be better to not live at all.

Yet now, with a little red star in his pocket, Roger felt he could go back to their home, and give his future a chance.

As long as he remembered: it was God's love for him that had brought Stella into his life when he had badly needed love, and help.

As long as he remembered: God loved him enough to remind him Stella's love still lived in him. Roger felt he could, if he wanted to, return to their home and find some joy in a future without Stella by his side. Then, one day, when it was God's timing and not his, he would be taken to join Stella in Heaven.

Roger was amazed that something so simple, something so small, could touch his heart enough to remind him to trust God to love him, to help him and to never leave him, even on his darkest days. With his hand in his coat pocket, Roger rubbed the little red star and smiled, a smile radiating peace, and because he remembered what love felt like, was happy to return home.

Dark nights and gloomy days: 'What happened to happiness and sunshine?' Keith grumbled as he walked towards the train station. *When did I stop laughing?* He could not remember finding life funny for a long time. *When did I stop smiling on my way to work? What has happened to me?*

He was working his way up the ladder in his chosen profession.

He was a fundraiser within an organisation, doing good in the community.

He was married to a wonderful woman, and shared two beautiful children with her. As Keith strode down the ramp to catch his train, his mind was filled with questions: *What is wrong with me? Why does every day look like there are never enough hours in the day for the amount of work I have to do? When did I think that I did not even have time for a lunch break?*

When did I begin to think that without me, the 'good' work would stop?

What happened to the laughing, carefree person I was when I started the job?

What happened to the person who believed there was always promise to the day—the person who looked forward to seeing what the day would bring?

When did I turn into this person who cannot see the sky is blue because my eyes never leave the pavement?

Even though he was only subconsciously searching for answers to the questions he heard in his head, Keith halted, mid-stride, when he saw something out of the ordinary.

What was that, that had glinted briefly in the sliver of sunlight? Probably would not have even seen it if I had not had to step out of the way of that last school kid.

Keith had just taken an involuntary step forward to keep his balance when he heard, 'Watch it, mate. Watch where you're going! You shouldn't just stop like that, you know,' a young executive in a pin-striped suit muttered. 'Darn dangerous to yourself and others, stopping like that,' the pin-striped suit added to his complaint, even while he continued to hurry to catch a train that had just pulled into the station.

Keith in return muttered 'Sorry' then read the number on the train and sighed. *My train!* Then, with a shrug of his shoulders, admitted he just was not up to the rush today. *Well, I am just not running for it this morning.* He watched the young 'pin-stripe' and the train leave the station then returned his attention to the glint of colour he had seen at the base of a steel column. *Now, what was that thing that caught my eye?*

Even as Keith bent to gather up the little golden star that had fallen behind one of the steel bolts at the base of one of the station's supporting columns, he began to be annoyed with himself. *I don't have time for this; I've already missed my train and the next one is due in any second.*

Still, he kept right on looking at the little golden star that was barely the size of his thumbnail. Turning it over, he caught sight of a little word written in white. Unaware of the hurried, jostling movements being made by impatient commuters all around the busy train station, Keith thought about the meaning of that one little word; let it settle into his mind and trickle down to his heart.

Happiness ... it had been a long time since he had last taken the time to remember to let happiness into his life. Happiness had been something he felt when he had given gifts to his family and friends. He could not remember when he had last given his lovely wife the gift she prized most—the gift of his time.

How long, he thought, *how long has it been since I have spent time with her? Not time running around doing things, or taking the kids somewhere, but actual time with her?*

Try as he might, Keith could not remember. *Maybe it was after the birth of our daughter ... surely it was not so long ago, was it?*

Their daughter, Beth, had recently turned ten. He had missed her party, just like the previous three, because the campaign he was working on had been due to start in three weeks, and was taking up all of his time.

But maybe I could have taken a couple of hours off and gone with her to the waterslide. It would have been an opportunity to meet her friends. I don't even know how many went.

Keith realised, not for the first time, that if someone asked him what Beth liked to do, or what her favourite colour was, or who her best friend was, he would not have been able to tell them.

When did I stop being involved in her life?

In another five years they would be financially set. Nine years ago, when he had set his target, he had been aware there would be many long days, and nights, of work needed to reach his goal. He had not made the decision on his own. No, they had talked about it. And he and his dear wife had agreed that after he had 'made it', reached the financial goal he said they needed for old-age security, they would have time to spend with each other, and the children.

Then, Keith remembered they had agreed, *then there will be time to do things with each other; time to do things with the children; time to go to the waterslide.*

Keith wondered whether at fifteen his daughter would even still want to go to the water slide. Mentally he groaned and thought, *Another five years …*

How will I survive another five years of not knowing my family, and not knowing myself?

Suddenly, Keith was swamped with a feeling of grief as he realised he missed the person who had enjoyed life, enjoyed his wife.

When did I turn into this person who is so work focused that there is never time for myself or my family?

In an effort to get himself back on track, Keith tried to give himself a pep talk. 'Still, it is only another five years of working fifteen hours a day, seven days a week.' The talk did not work.

Seven days a week, the words screamed through his head. *My God—when was the last time I took a day off to go to church? Was it Christmas? Easter? This year? Last year?*

It was no good. He could not remember clearly. He had grown up giving thanks to God for all his daily blessings. But now he could not remember when he had last taken time off work to spend time with his family, let alone allow time to celebrate God in his life. Keith felt his heart cry out, *What are you doing?*

Looking down at the tiny golden star glittering in the palm of his hand, he felt God speak to his heart and say, *It is okay; you have been busy and I have carried you in the palm of my hand, just as you are carrying this little star. You have never been alone. I never left you—but it's time, my precious boy that you took some time to seek ME again. It is time to reclaim your family; it is time to show them that there is joy in life.*

There is a time for everything, but you are not giving time to the important things in your life. If you came home to Me today, someone else would do your work. But if you came home to Me today, no one else could replace you in your family.

What is so important, Keith, that you would put your family second in your life?

Keith shook his head. Whether it was in answer to the question he heard or just to clear his mind, the undeniable fact was that the underlying sense of sadness saturating his life of late would not be shaken off. Knowing he could not go on as he had been, Keith ran to catch the train waiting beside the station platform, filled with people impatient to be on their way.

Keith made it into his office, gave his presentation on the new campaign, and then told his secretary that he was taking the rest of the day off.

Taking time off was something so unheard of that even his boss rang him to make sure Keith was okay. Keith simply said, 'I need some time with my family, for time is short and I am needed there.'

Then he headed out the door, caught the first train heading home, and ran all the way from the train station to his house. Slowing his pace only long enough to turn onto his garden path, Keith headed towards his house porch. He only stopped when he reached his front door, where he knew leadlight parrots would be reflecting onto the multi-coloured tiles of the hallway. Keith paused to really look at them, remembered the day his wife had picked them for the door, and realised he was smiling. Smiling as he had not done in a long time, and it felt good.

He unlocked the door and entered to stand quietly in the hall of their home. Hearing the key in the lock, his beloved wife of twelve years came out of the kitchen with a puzzled look on her pretty face, wondering why he was home. Without a word, Keith held out his arms as an invitation to her to join him where he was.

Her frown deepened with the concern she was beginning to feel, but still she accepted what her husband offered. It had been a long time since she had had such an invitation. Walking close, into his personal space, she found herself encased in her husband's arms. She did not know what had happened, or what had changed in his life, but she sighed and accepted the moment of firm, loving arms holding her. It had been a long time, and she wanted to savour the moment.

Keith breathed in the smell of her; it had been so long since he had taken the time to smell the essence of his wife. Then slowly he apologised. 'Forgive me. Please forgive me. I had forgotten what I was working for. I have forgotten so much, but mostly I forgot to love you. And I really do love you and our life together.'

Slowly, he took the little golden star out of his pocket and offered it to her with the writing side up, and simply said, 'I thought I'd lost it, but today God gave it back to me. He gave me back my happiness in my family, my happiness in Him, and my happiness in being alive. And you, my precious wife, are the best part of my happiness.'

She heard the wonder in his words, smiled and snuggled deeper into the arms of the man she had married, and gave silent thanks for his return.

She was alive and on her way home. Nicki's visit with her grandparents had been fun, until she had been bitten by a silly old wasp and had puffed up like a big balloon. It had taken days for the swelling to go away, and then it was time to go home.

She was supposed to have been asleep when she heard the doctor tell her grandma that they were lucky he had been in the area. 'Another few minutes, and the swelling would have cut off her airway and she would have 'asphyxiated'."

Grandma said that meant choked. Why the doctor had not just said choked, she did not know. Her mummy had caught the train up to Grandma's, and stayed for the rest of the week. Her daddy had rung, both morning and night, to tell her how much he loved her.

Now they were on their way home, and soon Nicki would see her friend Cindy again. It was such a shame that all of those lovely little, shiny stars Cindy had given her had been lost. Nicki had not even known the top of the bag had been open. She had cried when she had gone to show them to her grandma and discovered they were gone. Still, Cindy was a good friend, and she was sure Cindy would not be angry with her for losing such a good gift.

The train arrived at their station on time, and Nicki, impatient to get home, ran ahead of her mother. She was halfway up the ramp when she stopped. 'Hey, Mum,' Nicki yelled out. 'My shoelace has come undone. Can you please help me tie it up?'

Her mum, wheeling her suitcase, came alongside of Nicki and stopped beside her. To make it easier on herself, Nicki's mum lifted her onto the little ledge of the rock wall. After carefully retying the shoelace for Nicki, her mum began to lift Nicki down and back onto the ramp. At that moment, a tiny ray of sunlight danced its way through a hole in the roof and shone on something a little way along the ledge. Reaching out with her hand, Nicki gathered the shiny scrap of almost nothing into her hand and recognised it as one of her stars.

It was a pink one.

Nicki turned the little pink star over and saw a word written in white. Nicki smiled to herself and was happy because, just before the holidays, this word had been one of her spelling words. Nicki was happy, because she did not have to ask her mum to help her with the word, or its meaning. The word spelt 'friendship', and Nicki knew exactly what she was going to do with her little pink star. She was going to give it to her friend Cindy, then tell her all about her holiday and how glad she was to be home.

Why, Mummy, Why?

For Cooper, love always, Grandma Sue.

Jesus loves me, this I know,
For the Bible tells me so.
Little ones to Him belong,
They are weak, but He is strong.
Yes, Jesus loves me.
The Bible tells me so.

When the song ended, the Sunday school teacher smiled at all her little children as she released them from her charge. 'Remember that Jesus does love you, and He always will. Now go and find your parents, for now it is time to go home.'

Sally ran out of the room with her friends. If they were quick, maybe they could get to play for a little while. The rush to the door meant that everyone tried to get through at once. There was a little push and shove as they bumped into each other.

Sally's teacher was about to pull them all back into order when she heard the children softly laughing and teasing each other. She again smiled; the sound of happy children, and teaching them about God, were her greatest pleasures. The room emptied and she was alone. Closing her eyes, she thanked Jesus and prayed that each one of her children would truly know He loved them.

Sally, quickly but not very quietly, walked to find their parents in the big room where the preacher had held church. Sally was happy, because her mummy and daddy had stayed to have a cup of tea with their friends, so she had been able to play outside with the other children. However, too soon she heard her daddy calling for her. Amongst a chorus of goodbyes, Sally again found her parents and they all walked over to where their horse and cart was waiting.

Sally had really liked the last song they had sung in Sunday school, and while her mum settled her into the back of the cart, she began to hum its melody. Her dad gathered up the reins and talked to the horse. As soon as Sally heard the words 'gee-up' she held onto the rails of the cart. She knew that if she was not careful, when the horse moved she could be knocked off her seat by the jerk of the cart as it was pulled forward. Sally watched as the white wooden church and her friends became smaller and smaller the further down the road they went.

Soon she could not see them at all, but that did not bother her, because it was a beautiful day and she had lots of other things to look at. Her daddy drove the horse down the dirt road, through tall, white-trunked eucalyptus and iron-bark trees. Sometimes, Sally caught a sight of a small animal peeking out from under a shrubby bush. Soon they were travelling beside the creek and Sally recognised one of her favourite trees, the weeping willow. They only grew where the ground held moisture, but they were the best places to play hide-and-seek in, because their long, thin, leafy branches reached down and touched the ground.

Her baby brother, fast asleep, was tucked in his little carry-basket at her mother's feet. Sally was happy and she did love to sing and hum little tunes while she looked around. Her daddy was whistling along with her humming when, suddenly, Sally stopped humming and asked her mummy, 'Why does Jesus love me?'

Hearing her question, her daddy stopped whistling, and Sally wondered if she had asked a wrong question. Sally was six now, and although she asked questions all the time, she knew that there were wrong questions. Not wrong as in they should not be asked, but just wrong in when she asked them. Like the time Aunt Nora had come to stay, they had been sitting at the table ready to eat when, in front of the whole table, Sally had asked why Aunt Nora was eating with her teeth in today when she had not bothered with them the day before. That was when her mummy had told her that some questions were wrong questions to ask in front of other people. Some questions should be asked in private.

Swaying with the movement of the cart as it crossed a rock-built causeway, not hearing as the horse splashed through the water, Sally asked again, 'Why does Jesus love me? The song says it's because the Bible tells me so, but why, Mummy, why?'

Her mummy, leaning over to her to speak to Sally's daddy, suggested they stop to eat the lunch she had packed for them. Sally's mummy knew that this question, so innocently asked, was important and so not to be answered in a couple of words. The answer to this question needed her full attention.

Sally helped her mummy unpack an old blanket for the ground, while her daddy carried a heavy picnic basket into the shade of the trees by the creek bed. Sally waited patiently while her mummy settled her baby brother with her daddy by the picnic basket. Sally loved to climb up into her mummy's lap and be cuddled by her. For Sally, there was no safer place on Earth, unless it was on top of her daddy's shoulders when he carried her about the farm. But today her mummy had patted the blanket beside her, so that was where Sally sat.

After her daddy unpacked the food, and handed them both a drink, Sally's mummy said, 'Sally, I have been waiting for you to ask this question and, because it needs a long answer, I thought we might stop so that I can give you God's answer.'

'God's answer?' Sally frowned.

Her mummy gave her a little squeeze and said, 'Well, the answer to your question is in the Bible, just as the song says. It all started a long, long time ago, even before earth was formed. God lived in the Heavenly place. He had created living angels to be with Him. He created the angels to serve Him and to love Him. God divided His angels into three teams.

'One third He made into angels who carried God's messages, and He asked His angel Gabriel to look after them.

'Another third of his angels, God decided, would be ready to protect the other angels. So God called them His warriors, and He asked His angel Michael to be the leader of this group of angels.

'The remainder of the angels God called His singers, His worship team. These angels He put under the leadership of God's angel Lucifer.

'The leaders of the three teams of angels God called His archangels—his chief angels.'

Sally wiggled a little bit so that she could see her mummy's mouth telling the story. She loved to watch her mummy's mouth and see how it formed the words she said.

'For a long, long time the Heavens were filled with peace and love. All the angels seemed to be happy, but one of them was becoming dissatisfied with not receiving God's gratitude for the good job he was doing. Over time his dissatisfaction changed, and he began to think that not only should God recognise his worth, but all the other angels should as well.

'Lucifer had forgotten that God had created him along with all the other angels. Lucifer forgot that he only created music because God had given him the gift to sing. Lucifer forgot that God was God. So, Lucifer went to God and demanded to treat him the same as God.

'God was upset when Lucifer came to Him in this way. He said He had made Lucifer to lead the singing angels, but Lucifer was not the same as God. God could create, but angels could not. When Lucifer continued to insist that he was the same as God, God said there was no place in Heaven for angels who would not serve only Him. God had Lucifer thrown out of Heaven. Because Lucifer was their leader, a third of all the angels ever created, the music makers, followed Lucifer into darkness.'

Sally's mummy moved her fingers to place them under Sally's chin, and then tilted Sally's head so that Sally could see the honesty in her mother's eyes as she spoke to her. 'We today call this darkness

Hell, and know it to be a place of torment and pain because it is a place without God.'

Then Sally's mummy asked her a question that did not seem to belong with the story she was telling. "You enjoy having your friends come over to play and talk to you, don't you?'

Sally nodded her head in agreement, because she did indeed like having her friends over to play with her. Without commenting further on Sally's friends, her mummy continued her story.

'Well … although all angels can sing, God missed the ones He had created to bring music to the Heavenly places. God missed their beautiful voices and their songs of worship. Even though God had all the other angels to talk to, something was missing in God's life.

'And this, my darling girl, is where the Bible comes into our story, for God was lonely for a friend. He longed for someone who wanted to keep him company and talk to Him.

'So, God decided to create again. He decided that, this time, He would put the ability to choose in His creation. He would give His creation 'free will'. He wanted His creation to choose to be friends with Him, and not just spend time with Him because He had made them. This was a dangerous decision for God, because He knew that with the ability to choose, His creation could also choose not to be friends with Him.

'Before God could create a new friend, He needed to make somewhere for him to live. So He created the Heavens we see today. He filled them with the stars and the moon, and put that beautiful sun in the sky. Then He created Earth and put everything in it, including the animals of the land, the sea and the sky. He created the grass and the trees that we see here today.'

Sally's mummy, who knew her daughter liked to be involved with their storytelling, pointed to the branches way above their heads and said, 'Sally, God created this big tree we sit under today.'

Sally looked wide-eyed into the leafy branches above her head. Of course, she had heard that God created everything, but until just now she had never really looked and thought, *God made that.* Just then her baby brother cried out, and her mummy rose to go and see that her daddy was looking after him. Sally sipped at her drink, and waited. She knew that her mummy would be back to tell her more of her story. Sally was even a little bit excited, because she could reach out and touch a tree trunk that God had made.

Soon her mummy returned to sit on the blanket with Sally. Sally inched closer to make sure that she would hear every word her mummy spoke. This was exciting; learning about God and sitting by her mummy was always good.

'Now, precious girl, where were we … oh yes, I remember. When Earth was ready, with everything His new friends would need, God created first a man and then a woman.

'Sally, I know that you have heard of them, because you yourself told me that the Sunday school teacher talks about when God created Adam and Eve.'

Sally quickly nodded her head; she did not want her mother to stop the story.

'God enjoyed being his friends very much. He would come from the Heavenly places to walk and talk with them every day, and He was happy. But the fallen angel, Lucifer, was jealous that God had new friends. He did not want God to be happy. So he made plans to destroy God's friendship with Adam and Eve.

'The fallen angel thought that if he could get Adam and Eve to do something bad, then God would send them away, too. The fallen angel thought getting rid of God's new friends would make him happy, and God would be alone again.

'It was at this time that Lucifer, the fallen angel, became known to the world as Satan the deceiver. He is called this because of the plan he made to get rid of Adam and Eve. Satan planned to cause doubt in the minds of Adam and Eve about what God had said to them. In particular, Satan wanted them to question what God had really said about eating the fruit from a tree, in the middle of the Garden of Eden. Satan's plan was to play with the words of God's warning, and to tempt Adam and Eve to eat, and be more like God.

'Unfortunately, Sally, my darling girl, Satan's plan worked.

'Neither Adam nor Eve realised that they were already like God, because God had made them both in His image. They did not realise that when God created them, as well as giving them the gift of free will He put a little bit of Himself inside them. This is what makes people different to the angels.'

Sally's mum reached out and gently rubbed her fingers across the back of Sally's little hand, then continued with her story ...

'It is just as you know my touch, Sally, because you have a little bit of Mummy and Daddy inside you, inside your heart. When it is time for babies to be born, God puts a little bit of Himself in them so that, as they grow, they will recognise the touch of His love in their hearts. Everyone, everywhere has this little bit of God inside them. It hungers to know His touch yet waits for the people to make the choice to know God.'

Sally looked at her mummy and hoped with all of her heart that people would choose to know God, because if His touch was as good as her mummy rubbing her back, then they were all going to be very happy.

'The trouble was, Sally, Satan's plan worked. And Adam and Eve ate the apple from the tree. Suddenly they were dissatisfied with themselves. They realised that they were naked, and exposed to everything around them. They looked around the garden and saw everything differently, and they were no longer happy just to be in the garden.

'But the worst thing they did was, when God came that day to walk with them, they hid from him in the bushes. They knew they had disobeyed God and did not want Him to see them. Even though God knew where Adam and Eve were hiding, He gave them the chance to come to Him. He called out, "Adam where are you?" And He was sad.

'Not sad because they disobeyed Him. But sad they did not trust Him to forgive them. He wanted them to trust Him; He wanted them to talk to Him; He wanted them to know He loved them enough to understand that Satan had tempted them, and that He forgave them.

'God was sad because His friends now knew the difference between right and wrong, but they did not trust Him to forgive them. Instead, they were afraid that He would be mad with them, so they hid from Him. When he found them, they did not say, "We are sorry, please forgive us." All they could do was blame each other for eating the fruit. He told them they must leave the Garden of Eden and not return.

'It broke His heart, but because they did not tell the truth, and did not trust God to forgive them, they had to leave God's place. The difference between Lucifer leaving the Heavenly places and Adam and Eve leaving the Garden of Eden, was that God had hope in His heart for the children of Adam and Eve. His hope was that they would hear of God's love and choose to love Him back.

'God still loved Adam and Eve. He gave them land on which to grow food, and trees from which they could build shelters, to protect them from the weather. All this they had never had to do while living in the Garden of Eden.

'God watched Adam and Eve as they had a family. God watched as people multiplied and filled the land. He watched as they fought with each other over where to live, and he watched while they slowly forgot about Him.

'He did not want to be forgotten, for He missed spending time with His friends. So, from time to time, God would seek someone who was willing to hear Him. He would ask that person to tell the people about Him, in the hope that the people would remember God, and want to again spend time with Him. God was lonely; he loved all the people, and it hurt Him when the people did not want love Him.'

Sitting in the shade of the tree and slowly drinking the cold drink her daddy had brought to them, Sally's mummy continued to answer her daughter's question.

'God is patient, and God is good, and after many years watching His people forget Him, God asked the part of Him that we know as His Son, Jesus, to come to Earth, to be born as a human. God and Jesus knew that when Jesus became a man, some people would listen to the whispered untruthful words of Satan, and they would hate Jesus so much they would want to hurt Him. They would even want to kill Him.'

Sally could not help her question. 'But why, Mummy, why would they want to hurt Jesus? He did not hurt anyone, did he?'

Sally's mummy gently brushed Sally's curls away from her little face, and answered. 'No, darling, Jesus did not hurt anyone. He came only to tell of God's love for us. But the leaders of the church did not want everyone to know they could all talk to God if they wanted to. The leaders of the church wanted to continue to control the people, and the people's access to God's love, by letting them think that only the leaders could hear God.

'God knew the only way people would be able to hear of His love was if His Son, Jesus, came to Earth as a man to tell them. So, even though they both knew it would end in a horrible death, God still asked Jesus to come. And it did not stop Jesus. He willingly agreed to leave His safe, lovely place with God to come to live as a man. Jesus knew God's heart, and knew how much God wanted to share the people's lives again.'

Sally's mummy took her little face in between her hands, then, looking into Sally's beautiful brown eyes, she gave her daughter the best picture she could think of.

'Jesus came to Earth to grow from a baby, just like your little brother; to grow into a man just like your daddy; to love his mummy just like you do; to work for a living in a small village just like we do; until it was time for Him to leave His earthly home and family. When Jesus left His home, He walked from town to town, telling the people that God loved them.

'Jesus told the people that for them to know God, to show they loved God, they had to stop hurting each other, stealing from each other, and hating each other. He told them how God wanted the people to love Him, love each other, and treat each other better.

'The story of Jesus loving us is a sad one, and a happy one. It is sad, because some people were influenced by the fallen angel to kill Jesus; and it is happy, because we were able to hear about God's love, forgiveness, and acceptance. Jesus assured us that when He had gone back to live with God in

Heaven, we would never be alone. He told us God would send another part of Himself to Earth, to live with us and in us. We know this part of God to be His Holy Spirit. Jesus told us that once God's Spirit came, He would always be here to guide us, to strengthen us and to help us talk to God and Jesus every day—even all day if we wanted to.

'And that, my darling little girl, is how we know Jesus loves us.

'We know because He came. And He came because He loves us, as God, the Father in Heaven, loves us. When we talk about Jesus and His love for us, we must remember that Jesus did not stay in the grave. No. He is alive and well, and sitting at the right hand of God's throne in the Heavenly places.

'It was only in His living, dying and rising from the grave that Jesus exposed, and made powerless, all the lies Satan, the fallen angel, had built up over the years. Lies about how God had left us; lies about how awful we are; lies about each other, and lies about God.'

Knowing her story was almost told Sally's mother gave her daughter a hug and directed her words to answer the question she had been asked by her daughter.

'God knew we would need to know Jesus lived as we live. God knew that we would have to see Jesus' had a friendship with God before we would believe that we too could be friends with God. Jesus came to tell us God loves us and wants to be our friend.

'So, Sally, when you asked, "Why does Jesus love me?" I could do no other than to tell you the truth. Jesus loves you because God loves you. When you read the Bible it will tell you, in sixty-six books, that God the Father loves you; Jesus, who is part of God, loves you; and the Holy Spirit, who is part of God, loves you. You, dear one, could ask me how I know God loves me, and to answer that I will show you my favourite verse, which is John 3:16. It says, "For God so loved the world that He gave His only begotten Son, so that all who believe in Him will not perish but have everlasting life." For your mummy, Sally, that means an everlasting friendship with Jesus and God.'

Sally's mummy gave her a little nudge and helped her to her feet. 'So, my darling little girl, before we eat our lunch in this beautiful place that God made, let us go and ask your daddy to join us in singing your Sunday school song again. I can think of nothing better than singing, and remembering that Jesus does love us, and we know it's true because the Bible, the Word of God, really does tell us so.'

Author's Note

This story was inspired when my grandson was having a birthday and I did not know what to purchase for a present for him. I was reminded of Acts 3:2–6.

'Now a man who was lame from birth … when he saw Peter and John about to enter, he asked them for money. Peter looked straight at him, as did John. Then Peter said, "Look at us!" So the man gave them his attention, expecting to get something from them. Then Peter said, "Silver or gold I do not have, but what I do have I give you. In the name of Jesus Christ of Nazareth, walk."

And so, I could do no other than to give to Cooper what I have, the story of Jesus and His love for Him.

The Tabby and the Sheaf of Wheat

She was a little, silver-grey tabby, and she lived in the uppermost corner of the tower. She had come exploring many moons ago. She did not know how to count time; she had been a kitten when she arrived and now she was a cat. Her only interest in the days passing by was that in moonlight the tower was hers. With the rising of the sun, she had to move quietly and keep out of the humans' way. They did not like to see her walking through the rooms of the tower. They did not like to see her at all, even though she did a job she considered was hers.

She lived off the mice she caught and killed for food. Without her, the rooms of the tower would be overrun with mice. The tower was mostly empty of furniture and furnishings, but she knew that without her hunting skills nothing would have survived. *Mice chew and tear at everything*, she thought with distain.

The humans think the traps they set, and the few silly mice they catch, are what keep the tower from being overrun with mice.

As a kitten, her mother would box her ears and chastise her, because she had an adventurous nature. Then as her mother licked her ears clean, she would warn, 'One day, little one, you are going to adventure yourself right into trouble.' For many days after she had been accidentally trapped inside the tower, she had cried for help. When no help came, she explored and discovered an overgrown garden on the roof.

When it rained, water collected in the gutters, but even with the water she was growing weaker and weaker. Outside the tower, she had only learned how to jump on a grasshopper; mostly, she had just played with the animals her mother told her were food. Then the humans had set new traps and suddenly she had food to eat. She would watch the humans set the traps. By learning how to creep up on the silly mice, she began to catch her own supper.

She did, however, long for the company of her own kind, but because of the double set of doors she was afraid she would be trapped between the two. So she had resigned herself to never leaving the tower.

When the humans came, she would creep down the stairs and hide behind a chair to listen to their voices as they chatted about their day. She heard them congratulating themselves for keeping down the mice numbers in their tower. How she laughed, deep inside, when she heard the humans congratulate themselves for keeping the mice numbers down.

'We get the whole morning to clear out the mice, and it only takes half that to get around all the rooms in the tower. That means we get time to make a brew. I don't know what other keepers of the tower complained about.' The humans did not realise that she, and only she, was the reason the mice numbers were down, but they did not speak cat so how could she ever tell them the truth.

Then one day something changed. The humans dragged another human up the stairs, opened one of the uppermost rooms and threw him in. After locking the door, one had said, in a not very kind voice, 'There you go, see if you are able to rejoice now.'

She could not understand the actions of these humans, for she knew this room. There was nothing in it. Even the mice did not go in it. Until yesterday evening, there had been just bare stone walls and dust on the wooden floor. Then, just before dark, the humans had dragged up a bale of threshed wheat and thrown it in the corner. She knew it was wheat because she had played in it as a kitten. But it had been a long time since she had seen wheat, so she had spent the night hours sniffing at it, and poking at it with her paw, to try to understand why it was there.

Now she crouched low, in the shadows of the stairs, and watched as the humans closed and locked the door, leaving the other human lying on the wheat. She listened as the humans noisily made their way down the stairs. When she heard the big doors close, she crept over to the door. Still not sure what was happening, she kept low to the floor, and close to the shadows. Then she jumped onto a small ledge that ran around the walls of the corridor. After stretching, she extended to her extreme length and looked through the small opening in the door at the human inside.

He lay on the threshed wheat, looking at the ceiling, and seemed to be talking to himself. She could not hear what he was saying, but suddenly he sat up and held out a small head of wheat that had been missed in the threshing. Then the human said something she, as a cat, did not understand yet she knew she would never forget the moment.

She heard him say, 'You said, *I tell you the truth: unless a kernel of wheat falls to the ground and dies, it remains only a single seed. But if it dies, it produces many seeds. The man who loves his life will lose it, while a man who hates his life in this world will keep it for eternity.* Father God, I love You more than this life, and should You be able to use the ending of this life for Your glory, then I will rejoice.' Still puzzled, the tabby watched as the human placed the head of wheat on the shelf of his tiny window.

For many days and nights she visited the human's room, high in the top of the tower, and each time she saw him walking about his room and talking to himself. The humans brought water and food once a day, but did not talk to the man. The tabby did not realise when she had begun to separate her human from those who came and went every day. But every day she would look in on him, and in her mind she began to call him *man*.

Over time the man's appearance changed; she doubted that the humans would even recognise him as the person they had locked up. His fur grew long on his head and around his face. Each time she saw him she was puzzled, because he always seemed to be a little smaller than she thought he should have been. He was not walking as much as he first had; mostly she saw him just sitting, looking at the dried head of wheat on the window shelf. Often she heard him say the same thing over and over again. 'Father, please forgive them for they know not what they do.'

Who was he talking to, she wondered. *Who heard him?*

She had asked him once, but of course he did not talk cat and so he didn't understand. Instead, he had held out his hand and called, 'Puss, puss.'

It took her many moons to gather her courage, but eventually she had squeezed through the small opening in the door and gone over to him.

That was when she discovered the delights of having her ears tickled. Never before had she been touched in such a way; always she had been alone; always she had hidden from humans. Something in her changed when this man, locked away from his own kind, showed her kindness. Since that time, she had taken to checking on him at least twice a day, and each time she had been rewarded with a tickle.

One day, just as she had finished feasting on a big fat mouse that was not fast enough to escape her sharp claws, she heard the humans talking to each other as they made their way up the stairs to her man's room. They had carried something that was not food. She followed carefully, and then waited in the shadows outside her man's room. Even more puzzling was that the humans opened the door and went inside the room. This had not happened before. Sometime later, she watched as they dragged her man down the stairs, and deep into the dungeons of the tower.

She silently, and carefully, followed them down into the deep, dark, dank area beneath her tower. Of all the places in her tower, this was her least favourite. It stank so much down here that not even the silly mice came here. She watched as they threw her man into one of the rooms, closed the door with a loud bang, and made a fuss about turning the key in the lock.

After they had gone, she crept over to the door and tried to find a way in, but there was no access for her. All she could find was a small, two-inch crack under the doorway. Sitting in the damp outside the door, she turned her head sideways so that her ear was on the crack. Her heart dropped in her chest because, for the first time since her man had come to the tower, she heard the hopelessness of death in his voice. She heard his sobs as he cried out, 'Why, Father, why? Why have you forsaken me?'

She knew, even as she sent out her soft 'meow', that it would not reach through his despair. Day after day, she crept down into the bowels of the tower and tried to reach the man, but day after day, she left without him acknowledging she was there. She did not know that it was the deceiver of all things that was causing her man's despair. The words being whispered into his mind were taking away all hope of ever being rescued. She could taste his hopelessness, and she was saddened.

The humans, who brought him bread even the mice would not touch, did not come every day as they had before. Once, after they had peeped through the hole in the bottom of the door that the bread was pushed through, she heard them say, 'It will not be long now. Soon we will be digging a hole for him and can forget he ever existed. The rebellion against the King will stop, and no one will remember this man's warning about offending God.'

She watched them go, thinking, *There must be something I can do to bring some small hope back into the heart of my man.* Suddenly, there appeared a picture in her mind. And she could see her man as he had been, when he had first been brought to the tower. Without thinking anymore, she turned on her tail, raced up through the narrow dank alleyways, and up the stairs leading to the top of the tower.

Up, up, up she climbed; even the mice she would normally have chased stood still and watched as she raced past them. Up she ran, faster than she had ever run, until she reached the room she needed. Leaping lightly onto the cell's windowsill, she purred softly in satisfaction. Because there it was, the thing the man used to talk to: dried and shrivelled from resting within reach of the sun's rays, but still in one piece. She gently picked up the head of wheat with her mouth, then quickly but carefully returned to the dungeon cell. Very gently, she placed her precious gift at the base of the door, and nudged it with her nose until it was lying on the inside of the room. Then she sat down and called for him to notice it.

He ignored her, so she called louder. Still she heard no movement inside the cell. So she called more insistently. Still he did not come to the door. So she called to him as though she was in pain, and indeed she was, for she could feel his pain in the very heart of her. She heard him say, 'Go away, puss.'

It was not much, but it was something, so she called more urgently, and again he said, 'Go away, puss, there is nothing here for you. The end has come and all hope is gone.'

Again she called out her pain for him to hear, and eventually she heard him move; crawl towards the door. She knew the exact moment he found her gift. For there was a silence so full of emotion that she thought, just for a moment, she could see the air around it glowing from the crack under the door. The tabby frowned and lifted her head in surprise, but it was gone before she would even be sure that the light had been there. Then, in the silence, she waited. Her wait this time was different from before, because this time she expected her man to talk again. She breathed very shallowly as she did not want to miss his voice. But it was not words she heard; he simply cried.

When he stopped crying, his breath came in long sighs. Wondering whether he was all right, she crouched down, alert for any sound, and waited while her human snuffled as he drew air deep into his lungs. After some time had passed, she heard him say, 'Oh Father, I had forgotten. I had forgotten You would keep Your promise to never leave me. Forgive me, for I was blinded by my suffering, and could not see past the cold and damp. But You *are* here, and I am Yours. Thank you for puss, and her gift.'

Just then, she heard them coming. She heard more humans than had ever come to the dungeons before. They were loud in their coming. She could hear creaking, and the banging of doors as they checked all the rooms. They were loud in their voices as they called to each other. She shrank back into the darkness to hide from the searchers; from the shadows of the dungeon walkway, the tabby saw they had reached her man's door and were even louder in their irritating calls. She did not know they were shouting with joy …

'He is here, he is here. Bring the robe.'

'Bring water.'

'Come help me lift him.'

One of the humans wrapped the shrunken, weak form of her man and whispered, 'The King, your uncle, is dead. Your brother is the new King. He has had the whole army searching the land for any sign of you. He is waiting to hear that Our God has been merciful and that you are alive.'

They carried her man away; she watched them go.

For many days after they had taken him, she would go down into the damp, dark dungeon looking for him. But he was gone. Eventually she stopped looking and went back to chasing, and catching, the silly mice, which tried to build a home in her tower. She never forgot her man, but he took less of her time as the days passed. Indeed, many days passed and she did not even think about him.

Then, one particularly bright, sunny day the front doors of her tower were pushed open and in came a lot of noisy humans. She watched them from the shadows of the stairway to see what they were going to do. She was surprised when all but one turned and left the room, closing the door as they left. She cautiously watched in case it was a trick, as humans had tried to catch her before, so she stayed very still and watched from her hiding place.

Suddenly she heard it, a soft warm voice calling, 'Puss, puss, puss.' Over and over, the gentle voice of her human called to her. She suspected it to be a trick because she knew her human had gone away, so she stayed still and silent. After a short pause, she heard his voice calling her again. Still wary, she watched as the human took off his shining helmet. With the human's head exposed, she recognised him to be her man. He sat in the middle of the black-and-white tiles of the tower's entrance hall, and waited. He did not look as though he were impatient to be gone from the tower, which made her wonder, *What could he want?*

The man sat very still, and gently called out to her. He knew she was shy, and very wary of humans and what they would do if they caught her. He had come to tell her that she had nothing to be afraid of. She had saved his life. He had been dying, he had lost hope in his spirit, he had lost his will to live, and she had given it back to him. Just before he was rescued from prison, she had brought him a gift. The gift had reminded him of his faith, of his promise to trust in God to be in control of every situation, even during war.

And so now he was here to thank her. But would she trust him enough to come to him? He would give her the opportunity to come and live in a different part of the castle, but he knew she would probably stay in her tower with its overgrown rooftop garden and her constant war with the mice.

So he sat quietly in the middle of the huge entrance hall, and gently called to her. She had spent many hours outside his cell door, calling to him to live. So he would sit and pray that she would be curious enough, brave enough, to investigate the man who called to her. After what seemed like a long time, he was rewarded. He saw her move out of the shadows and creep closer to him. He reached out his hand and waited. He knew deep within his heart she would never ask much from him. She was too independent, and had lived alone for too long to need anything from man. But he would do all he could to answer whatever need she had. He had thought to bring her a kitten, to see if she would like some company, but that was for another time because this time, the first time, was his time to thank her. So he waited, knowing she would come because she enjoyed a tickle, and the time it took to give her a small tickle, and a few gentle pats, was nothing in comparison to the gift she had given him.

When Hope Survives

For Jessie Bell – thank you for
sharing your love of the bush.

The sun rose over the horizon, sending forth rays of light to filter through the branches of the gum trees surrounding her home. Silently they came, reaching in through an open window, stretching to bring light to even the darkest corner of the room. She knew immediately the moment the rays of light had climbed from the floorboards to scatter her sleep and bring awareness that another day had begun. Her long years of rising with the dawn, and setting a fire in the big, black kitchen range in readiness for another day, had set the pattern of her sleep. She could feel the dryness of the day beating down on the land, even before her feet touched the floor.

Slowly, she left her place of rest, mindful that nothing would probably change today, but still, in her heart of hearts, she hoped that rain would come.

Wordlessly she hoped, prayed, begged, that somewhere storm clouds were building. She hoped these clouds would come to answer the call of the land, and to fill her dams, fill her water tanks. The hope she held was, briefly, fed by the zebra finches as they cheerfully, cheekily, flew in and out of her bedroom windows, calling to her to *come fill our water dish*, calling her to *come fill our seed bowl*.

She thought, *Is this a message for me; an answer to my heart's cry? These little birds wake in the morning knowing that they will find what they need to survive, when they need it. Is this the message, God, to trust You to provide in time, on time, what I need when I need it? But then, You know that I do worry, and I will continue to worry, just as every other farmer on the land worries.* She shook her head at her imaginings. 'Get a grip, old woman. How many times have I had to tell you that hope is a strange thing that it takes hold of any little thing and builds on it? Do I have to remind you how often hope has let you down? Now look what it's done; you're talking to yourself again."

After dressing, Tess shuffled down her vinyl-covered hall, and heard the silence of the house waiting to be awakened for the day. Opening a small kitchen window, Tess reached for a box of matches she kept on the sill. After adjusting the flue on the chimney of her cast-iron, woodburning stove, Tess lifted the cover off its front hob, struck a match and carefully lowered the flickering flame through the opening. Carefully, she moved the fragile flame around the edges of a nest made of old newspaper. Inside this nest, very carefully stacked the evening before, a reward to the fire for staying alive, was a small stack of dry twigs.

As the newspaper began to blacken and curl from the heat of the flame, Tess leant down and gently blew on the dormant promise held within the paper. She watched to see the paper sacrifice itself to feed the flame. Tentatively, the flame flickered around the small stack of dry twigs resting with the now blackened paper. Blowing again, Tess was reassured that her job was done when the flames boldly discarded the blackened paper and began to feed on the twigs.

Straightening, Tess turned to gather a handful of hardwood splinters, and then fed them, one by one, through the open hob. Tess paused after inserting each piece to ensure the burning twigs would take the weight of the denser wood. After a few minutes, Tess placed her water-filled, oversized black kettle over the open hob. As soon as it boiled, Tess would make her first cup of tea for the day.

Automatically, Tess opened the fire-pit door and, with a cast-iron poker, stirred the fire before adding some larger pieces of cut firewood. While waiting for the kettle to boil, Tess straightened and rubbed her back. Her face a little flushed from the heat of the fire, Tess turned toward the slight breeze slipping through the open window. Gazing out, looking through the grapevine growing over her back-door trellis, Tess lifted her eyes to the morning sky, thinking, *I know you see the bigger picture, but oh God, this drought is driving people from the land, and the worry about paying for trucking in water is just so emotionally draining. I don't know if I have enough in me.* Tess finished her thoughts by expelling a sigh of acceptance. *Well, there is nothing I can do about it. I am here until I am gone ...* The strident whistle of steam being pushed up the spout of her kettle was a happy distraction for Tess.

After filling a cup from her favourite, age-battered, silver-coloured teapot, Tess walked through her house to stand at the edge of her front veranda and drink in, not only her cup of tea but also messages from the bush. Slowly, listening to the awakening bush, Tess sipped her tea and again, silently, pondered where the rain was.

This was a favourite place for her, a place where she could see the mountains in the distance as well as the beautiful bush trees surrounding her home. Tess remembered other times when she had stood in exactly the same spot, with one or other of her children and grandchildren. Each of them knew that when they came to her for advice, she would speak the truth. And she would always remind them that God would not give them a load too heavy to carry without giving them the strength, and the wisdom, needed to have victory over their problems.

Tess was not a particularly religious person, but she knew that she had only survived her own trials by holding fast to her belief that there was a God, and that He would help her through all her rough times. And, over her many years, He had.

Knowing she could not be overheard, Tess admitted the things that were sitting heavy on her heart.

'The rainwater tanks are nearly dry. Yes, I know, they have been dry before, but I am only human, and not as young as I was. To be honest, I don't even know whether I will be here to see the rain when it comes. This drought has been going on for six years, and, I have to admit, I am worried about it. Oh, I know, rain has always come in the nick of time to top up the dams and the tanks, but these last years it has never been enough to refill the underground reservoirs, or really nourish the ground.'

Leaning against the railing of her veranda, Tess felt every one of the many years she had spent on Earth. She felt wearier than she had ever felt. Even telling herself that God was in control did not lift the heaviness from her heart.

Each evening Tess went out and tapped the side of the house tanks to find the depth of water in them. Last night the hollow sound, indicating there was no water at that level, had stopped just three finger-widths above the brass tap. The small dam her man had put in to supply washing water to the house was down to mud; her precious veggie gardens were nothing but dust and withered weeds. Just remembering her gardens brought regret and a touch of bitterness to her thoughts.

Tess thought about the time and effort she had put into carrying buckets of water from the dam, trying to save the plants in her market-garden beds. It had come to nothing. She had been able to protect the plants from hungry animals by using wire netting, but saving them from being eaten was not the same as trying to save them from drought. So Tess had turned her efforts to the small garden she had planted for her own use. Once it had supplied her with corn, peas, lettuces, strawberries and other sweet treats. Every spare drop of water had been poured into it, but all it did was disappear through the ever-widening cracks around the plants' roots without ever touching the plants themselves.

In the end it all just got too hard; the more she tried to keep going the more she saw how little effect she had. Still, every morning she rose to try again, and every day her heart hardened a little more against the hope of a miracle. The beauty of watching kangaroos, wallabies and even the odd wombat come in to drink was spoilt now by the pain it caused her when she had to chase them away from the dam.

That water was her life!

She had to fight for that water to survive. There was no longer enough to share. Even though it broke her heart, she had to chase them away, make them hop away. Hop to find what moisture they could find around the base of moss-covered rocks in the once strong-flowing riverbed only two short miles over the hill.

Her man was away, yet again. Even in drought, sheep grew wool and shearing went on. They both knew he was getting too old to be dragging and clipping sheep all day long; neither of them would see seventy again. Both of them knew he had only a limited amount of time left to work the sheep. Once he had travelled half the state as a gun shearer, but now he only worked in the local area.

Tess, remembering it was Friday, was pleased the weekend was around the corner. Her days ran into each other without much change, but at least at the weekends her man was home to help with the chores.

Standing sipping her tea, Tess reminded herself that it would be good to have another living soul in the house for a couple of days, although the last time he was home he had indulged in too many 'Mungandai shandies'. It was his favourite, and he made it by mixing brown Muscat wine with beer.

She had tried to tell him to take it easy, but he knew best. He would forget that, with age, the body did not process alcohol as well as it did when it was younger. She wished he listened to her, because the potency of the brew got to him. He did not do it all the time—drink until his feet forgot to work— and he never hurt anyone but himself. It had nearly broken her back when she had tried to help him up the steps and into the house. It did not matter that it was a foolish thing he had done; she had not been able to leave him to lie like a broken doll at the foot of the back steps.

Tess acknowledged that she cared for him, even after fifty-two years of marriage, although she could have killed him herself when, two months ago, he had been pulled over and booked for drink driving after a trip to town. A lifelong habit of visiting the Tats hotel after shopping was making the return trip from town scary and dangerous. Her worry about having an accident through having 'one more for the road' was put aside because she would use the time to visit with her sister while he was with his mates.

Tess had never learnt to drive when she was younger and now it was too late. The neighbours had been good in helping her get into town to buy groceries, but they only went to town every two weeks. Because they were kind enough to take her,

Tess did not like to ask for an extra half-hour so she could visit with her sister.

Leaning on the doorpost, looking out at the bush surrounding her home, Tess had to wonder whether the solitude of the bush was finally closing in on her. In her youth, she had willingly made her home surrounded by the beauty of tall, grey-green eucalyptus trees, and the animals of the bush. Recently, she had found it harder not to see another friendly face from one week's end to another. The isolation of having neighbours miles away, and out of earshot, had been easier to handle when she knew that at the end of the week there would be a trip to town for supplies.

Death is a fact of life, and normally she was able to deal with it, but the death of two long-time neighbours, and friends, had been more difficult for her this time.

Lost in her thoughts, Tess did not notice the sun as it rose higher in the sky, changing the soft morning glow into the harsher light of another hot day. The beauty of her bush was, for that moment, lost on Tess as she questioned aloud, 'Am I scared because my time is nearly over, or just sorry that I am still here to think about these things when so many of my friends are gone?'

Tess had come to the house as a child bride, but *maybe it is time to leave. The house needs some repair work done on it, not much, but time is beginning to tell on it; even the kitchen garden is too hard to handle alone. Maybe the children are right: maybe it is time to move to town where life would be easier.*

Tess knew from visiting her sister that, in town, the electricity was connected to the houses and turned on with a flick of a switch; it was so much easier than fighting with her generator each evening to bring light to the house, and power to her television set.

In town, hot water was just a turn of a tap handle away; she would not have to heat water for her bath on the stove, or light the copper for her weekly wash. There was much to say about moving to town, but there were things she would miss as well, like washing her hair in the open air using a dish by the tank stand, and sipping her first cup of tea watching the bush come to life each morning.

But to flick a switch and turn on a tap ... maybe they were right, and now is the time to move. Move to a place where I would no longer have to fight the animals of the land for life-giving water. When the rain stays away it is easy to accept I am tired, so bone-weary tired with trying to survive.

There was no doubt Tess would miss the place. She had raised her children here. Over the years she had survived other droughts, floods and even bushfires when they had ravaged this land that was hers. She had killed snakes that had tried to invade her space, and handfed lambs left motherless for one reason or another.

Despair filled her heart when she silently questioned: *How can I leave?*

She had helped to scrape a living from the land by trapping and skinning rabbits while waiting to harvest wheat from their paddocks. She had worked alongside her man in the shadowed corner of their corrugated-iron shed extracting honey from the beehives. She had spent long hours searching through the wash-heaps of abandoned tin mines. Tess looked, hoping to find pieces of tin too small to be noticed by the original miners. Tess knew the tin was sold by weight, so patiently she had collected the tiny pieces of heavy black stone. She would store her treasure in empty jam jars and powdered-milk tins until she had enough to sell.

Memories flooding her mind—not all good, but not all bad either—were hers and hers alone.

She had been glad when her days as the shearer's cook had finished. The days had been long, starting before daybreak and not finishing until after dusk. Cooking food for eight men in that oven they called a kitchen had drained the life out of her.

Her eyesight had faded rapidly in the last two years; some silly thing that could not be corrected by man had clouded her sight and sapped her confidence. Tess knew she still moved easily around the well-known areas of her home, but out in the world, out of her comfort zone, she was slow and unsure of herself. Even the odd trip to town had become an ordeal because the items in the shops were now unrecognisable without close scrutiny, and people had no familiarity until she heard them speak. It had been hard for Tess to acknowledge, and even harder still to accept, that the years she had lived had finally caught up with her.

Her body was tiring, but at times the girl inside still wanted to dance and sing. But not today: today there was no dance in her. Tess knew she was nearly ready to accept the change that had to come. Her independence was something she valued, but the time was coming when she would need help. But the thought of what that might mean scared her; she did not know what the future would bring, or how she would handle being away from her beloved land.

Standing on the veranda's edge sipping her first cup of tea, listening to black-and-white magpies call out messages in song, she glanced at the sky and frowned. Something was different, felt different. Something had changed; the air itself seemed different somehow. Tess looked around with her hazy gaze and strained to see the change …

Is that a bit of smudge on the horizon? Is it dust? Is it … Puzzled by the 'hope' she heard in her wayward thoughts, Tess dismissed them as just wishful thinking. *No, it's just me hoping that today God will answer an old woman's prayers.*

But then her heart caught up with her thoughts and she paused to give them value. Her age-softened brow creased into a frown of concentration. *Wait ... there ... that light breeze ...*

Lifting her head, closing her faded blue eyes, Tess remained as still as she could and allowed herself to smell the air, taste the air. And there it was. Tess felt a tiny change in the air. The hairs on her body reacted to the word that went with the change.

So focused was Tess on identifying the change, she could have been mistaken for a statue. She was searching her memories; somewhere, sometime, she had seen this before. A thought came, but she pushed it back, so afraid that she could be wrong Tess barely breathed. Then, there it was, as clear as anything she had ever seen. The image that matched the word, the word she had pushed aside— water-heavy clouds, clouds building above the hills. And the change she had felt was a promise to be fulfilled.

Tess looked harder at the horizon, struggling to match her remembered image with reality, felt her heart, not completely hardened by a life of striving to survive in the Australian bush, flutter in her chest. Suddenly she felt all the hope she had been repressing, the hope of farmers everywhere, to grow ... just a little ... and prayed.

Maybe today the rain will come to bring life back to the land—maybe today I will not have to decide to leave this land I love.

God willing, maybe today the rain will come.

Miracles Do Happen

And so, as she sat beneath the big old gum tree at the bottom of her garden that seemed to stretch on until forever, her thoughts strayed to the little boy who had wandered into her house, and the man who had come looking for him.

How could I have done it?

She must have scared him half to death. If the truth be known, she herself had not really known what was happening to her. Ellie had been walking from the sitting room to find her daughter in the kitchen when the boy appeared inside her front door. At first she had thought that she was going a little mad. There was no earthly way a boy, who was the image of her son Edward, should be where this boy was. Then he had moved and Ellie had literally expelled her breathe in a loud, agonising groan and fainted.

Hearing the extraordinary sound followed by a 'thump', Sonya had come running from the kitchen and Edward from the library. Sonya had run to her mother, while Edward had been quick enough to catch the boy before he disappeared back out the open door. Ellie remembered thinking, *Thank the Lord they caught him before he had a chance to slip out the door, and possibly out of our lives, before we could find out who he was.*

'My pa,' he had said, 'is outside seeing to the horses. I was supposed to stand still out of the way until he was finished. But the front door was open and I just wanted to take a peep inside. I didn't mean to come all the way in.' Then, with what seemed to be a practised gambit, the boy began to take the focus off himself. 'It sure is a big house …' The rest of his words died in his mouth, and he tried to pull away from Edward's grasp just as Ellie's beautifully carved wooden front door swung inwards.

A man who looked as though he was used to working in the open air stepped forward, calling the boy to come to him. Just as the boy's words had died on his lips, so too did the words being spoken by the man. Ellie was sure that the reasons were poles away from being the same. She could see the man assess the scene in front of him. It must have looked extremely odd. There was an overweight, fifty-year-old woman being helped up from the black-and-white tiled floor by a younger version of the woman. A tall, broad-shouldered young man, in his mid-twenties, was holding tightly to a squirming boy, who just happened to be the man's son.

Sonya felt her mother, who was now thankfully standing by her side, become rigid in her stance, so she turned to see what her mother was looking at. Edward, when he felt the boy cease his struggles, also looked towards the newcomer. As each of her children saw who had entered, they stilled and stared in astonishment. They could have been looking into a mirror, with the exception of minor details, as each of them saw themselves in the newcomer.

The newcomer was the first to recover from his silence, and although he spoke with confidence, Ellie could hear his need to uncover the reason why, in appearance, he resembled the people in this room.

'Sorry,' he apologised. 'I had asked Tom to stay on the veranda while I tended to the horses. Guess I should have known an open door, and a turned back, would be too much for him to resist.' As though he was a little afraid to stop talking, the man in the doorway hurriedly added, 'My name is Jack, by the way. We have recently moved to the neighbourhood. We bought the old McIntoshes' place down the road. Not a bad little place, a bit rundown, but me and the boy, we'll set it right in no time at all. We were on our way home from town and thought we would call in and introduce ourselves as new to the neighbourhood.'

And through it all no one moved; they all just stared at him and wondered, *What?*

What could one wonder when the man looked like he belonged at their dining room table.

She could see the questions running through the heads of her children ....

Who is he?

Where did he come from?

And how can he look like us?

Even as she read their thoughts as they raced around her children's heads, her own were just as jumbled.

What can I say?

My God, who are you?

Where are your parents?

Where do you come from?

How old are you?

When is your birthday?

Are you adopted?

Are you my missing baby?

Hello, I'm Ellie, your mother, and these are your siblings.

But she had said none of these things.

Ellie had, again, inelegantly passed out on her oh-so-clean tiled floor. After regaining her senses with the help of her son's strong right arm, she had struggled to stand, then, insisting she would be better after some fresh air, rushed from the room. Ellie's intention had been to secure a few moments to collect her thoughts before answering the questions she knew were waiting for her.

It was not until Ellie had reached the end of her garden that she realised she had left a ticking bomb in her entrance hall. Still, Ellie knew there was no way she could go back into the house until she had gathered her thoughts. And so here she was, sitting in the shade of the gum tree in her backyard, being forced to think about a time many years ago. A time when part of her heart had been ripped out of her chest. That time … the time when she given her baby up for adoption.

Oh, how she had cried, but not out loud. Her tears of loss had to remain hidden; she 'had done the right thing', and was supposed to 'forget it happened', 'get on with her life'; everyone thought it was for the best. And she tried. She really had tried, but there were times when her eyes filled, and her sadness flowed silently down her cheeks.

If only the government had not had that ridiculous way of choosing who would go to fight for another country's freedom, and who would stay home. 'By birthdate!' Ellie snorted her disgust. 'I suppose those whose birthday fell outside the parameters were happy. I was very unhappy.'

Her Derrick, her wonderful Derrick, had been sent to Vietnam, and he had not even known about the baby. Ellie had not been part of the 'flower power' people. She had only loved Derrick, and they had been planning to marry. Even though, at the time, 'freedom loving' girls were choosing to have their babies or not, society rules in a small rural township dictated the order in which families were formed. First the courtship, then the marriage, then the babies.

Ellie's family had been shocked, upset and worried about the shame she was bringing on them. They had talked about not allowing her to have her baby, but because she became sick even thinking about aborting, they had considered other options.

Ellie remembered, when she had been a child, sitting quietly in the corner of the kitchen when her mum and Aunty Merle had spoken softly about the shame a young girl in their neighbourhood had brought on her family. Hurt and shame, and all because a baby had not been planned.

Ellie had not understood why you had to plan a baby. *Didn't God bless people with babies, didn't the teaching at Sunday school talk about how God had blessed mankind with His son through Mary, and she had not been married. Well, not to start with anyway.* When Ellie had tried to talk to her mum about this, her mother had shushed her, and told her God's Mary was the exception. 'Young girls do not have babies until they are married.'

There had been nothing more said in front of Ellie about unwed girls and unplanned babies. Through the years that followed, Ellie had not thought any more about the conversation she had overheard. That was until the ache in her heart had formed. Since that time, Ellie had watched, with a hurting heart, and seen more and more unwed girls keeping their babies.

But back then, it had been Ellie who had been pregnant, and her family had been unable to deal with the shame, so in the end they had sent her to stay with Aunty Merle in South Australia until the baby had been born and put up for adoption.

Ellie knew it might have been different if the telegram had not come. It had been the telegram that no one, with someone away fighting, wanted to receive. The telegram went to Derrick's parents, and told them Derrick was missing in action. Everyone in their town had prayed that Derrick was still alive and would be coming home, but after a couple of months the world moved on, and people began to believe missing in action meant dead.

Ellie had continued to pray, and believe he was alive, but the only people who would talk to her about Derrick's survival were his parents. Ellie had been slow in showing her pregnancy, but even so, as soon as she had started to look pregnant, her parents had moved her to her Aunty Merle's.

Ellie stayed with Aunty Merle for four months. Six months after her return home, only a couple of weeks before Christmas, her prayers were answered. Derrick's parents had another letter from the army. This word brought with it news worthy of celebrating. Derrick had been found in a village miles away from where his patrol had been fighting. He had been captured, and was being taken, by the enemy, for interrogation when friendly natives had attacked the enemy patrol and rescued him. He had been hurt in the fighting, and his rescuers, not knowing where to take him, had taken him to their village to help him heal.

Derrick happily confirmed this story when they shipped him home. He had lost his memories through his injuries, and not recovered them until friendly soldiers had entered the village where he was staying. And so he had come home, home to his sweet love, and they had been married at Easter.

No one knew about the hole that resided in her heart. Ellie had never had the heart to tell Derrick about the baby. She knew he would have torn the world apart to find some trace of his baby. And she had promised everyone she would never try to find the baby; they had made her sign papers saying she would never look for him, never try to claim him. It was best for the baby, they all said so, and it was best for her.

And so Ellie had kept silent, never talking about the part of her that was missing, never letting anyone know she celebrated her baby boy's birthday each year with a strawberry malted milkshake. Ellie had never told anyone of her secret yearning to one day know whether or not he had survived.

Then last year her Derrick had died. Gone home to be with the Lord, and she had wondered whether now would be the time to seek some answers. Ellie really had not meant to disturb her baby's life, just find out whether or not he was okay. And even as she had tried to find out where to start, Ellie had heard the testimony in church of a family reunited after forty-five years.

She had heard how, after years of looking for their daughter, they had opened their hearts to God. Ellie had listened while they told how they had asked God to open the way to reunite their family, and then had let Him do the work.

Ellie had heard how hard it had been for them to not be actively looking for their missing daughter, but they had to trust their prayers would be answered. She heard how the family had remembered Joseph, in the Old Testament of the Bible, who had been sold by his brothers, but years later God had reunited them. Not only had God reunited the brothers, but He also opened up their hearts so they had a good family relationship.

So Ellie had knelt beside her bed, opened her heart to God, and let Him reach into all the places that had hurt for so long, as she had asked for news of her baby boy. Then she had left her request with God to work on, and in doing so, honoured all the promises she had made not to track her baby down.

That had been two months ago yesterday, and today she had driven into town to have a strawberry malted milkshake.

'God, give me the strength and your wisdom to deal with the questions inside my house,' she whispered, before returning to face the questions she knew were waiting for her. Ellie was surprised to realise that her time outside must have been shorter than she had thought, because inside no one had moved. All of her children were still warily looking at one another. Young Tom, completely oblivious to the tension in the room, was pulling on his dad's hand and asking for a drink.

As she entered the room, Jack turned to her and tilted his head, just as his father had always done when he was seeking answers to silent questions. The resemblance to her Derrick removed once and for all any doubt she may have had that this was indeed her long-lost baby come home to visit.

What is he asking in his silent look?

How could I know?

Then, just as suddenly, she knew; knew he was asking, 'Is it true?'

Are you real?

Could it really happen like this?

And she nodded to him and smiled a small smile, asking in her own way, *Can you forgive me? Can you accept me – us?* Ellie knew she was telling him with a small smile that she wanted him to know who she was.

Sonya and Edward, even though puzzled by the appearance of the newcomer, stood together, as though to gather sibling strength in order to deal with the news they guessed was coming. And Jack—Ellie could see that Jack was still trying to comprehend that, maybe, these people were not the strangers he thought they were.

Ellie turned to her daughter, and asked her to go to bring some refreshments for everyone, before indicating they all go into the sitting room. 'Jack,' she said, as she extended her hand, 'my name is Ellie, and I have a story to tell you.' Ellie waited until Sonya returned with a freshly cooked Madeira cake with orange frosting, freshly brewed coffee and an apple juice for Tom before sharing her story. When she had finished, Ellie sat back and waited.

Jack, having already had time to look from person to person, heard Ellie's story and was able to accept the truth of it. The resemblance between Ellie and her children was exceptionally close. In the same way, the resemblance he and his son had to the three people in the room could not be denied. Then, glancing down at his son, he shared a story of his own.

His story was of a wonderful, loving couple who, unable to have children of their own had, thirty-two years ago, been given the gift of a healthy baby boy. They had just about given up hope of ever having a baby to call their own, as they were then in their early forties.

Ellie heard that Jack's childhood had been one of love and security, good schooling and parents who believed in bringing up their child in the ways of the Lord God. And so he had grown through the usual years of childhood, into his teens and into adulthood, where he had met, and married, a wonderful woman.

Jack told them how they had worked together on the family farm, until his wife and both of his parents had been taken home to Heaven in a car accident. This had all happened less than two years ago, before Tom's fourth birthday. Jack told them how he had struggled with the loss of his loved ones. Told them how he had been angry with God for taking them from him.

Eventually Tom's needs, and God's peace, had finally reached into his heart and healed his hurt. He still missed his family every day, but now he was committed to ensuring Tom received the love and guidance he himself had received.

'It had taken some time, but I realised that it was time to accept that we were still a family, even though there were only two of us. I talked to Tom and we decided to start afresh, in a new place. So after selling the farm we searched the web to find somewhere that sounded good, and we found the McIntoshes' farm.' Looking down into his son's upturned face, Jack smiled and added, 'Didn't we, mate?' Tom nodded his head in agreement as his dad continued.

'Although the place was rundown, and would need a bit of work, it felt right so we decided to give it ago. We have been camping out in the house, doing a bit of clearing out, before our furniture arrived yesterday.'

Jack's next words had Ellie's eyes opening wide in surprise.

'Tom and I share a birthday, and we both love strawberry malted milkshakes. So we went into town to celebrate our birthdays with a 'shake. It has become a bit of a tradition for us, hasn't it, Tom?' Tom again was quick to agree with his dad. 'Anyway, we thought, seeing as how we were riding right past your gateway, that we would call in and introduce ourselves as your new neighbours.'

Jack, turning to Ellie, paused a moment before adding, 'After the accident, after the shock, I too offered up a prayer to Jesus. I prayed that if it was His Will then I would like to meet my birth mother. My adoptive parents always encouraged me to think of the courage, and the strength, my birth mother must have had to be able to let me go. I did not understand how hard it must have been for her to do that, until I held my own son for the first time.'

Ellie, aware of how Tom wriggled and squirmed as he tried very hard to sit still, brought out some of Edward's old toys for him to play with. Jack seemed to embrace the idea of being part of a family again. Ellie could see both Edward and Sonya were processing the prospect of a future with a brother they never knew existed. By the smiles they sent Tom's way, there was no doubt that they would be pleased to have a nephew to love and, maybe, spoil just a little.

Ellie took a moment while others shared bits of their life, and silently thanked God for restoring to her what was lost. She thanked Him for the blessing Jack had been to his adoptive parents, and for the future God had planned, so many years ago, even before Jack had been born.

It could have been so different. Ellie was aware of what the world could do to people. She knew that not everyone treated their children with love respect. Ellie saw and heard, every day, how horribly some parents hurt their children, yet God had protected and blessed her baby.

Ellie also asked for God's forgiveness for not sharing Jack's existence with her Derrick. Her excuse was it had been too hurtful, and, if she was truthful, she had been ashamed because she had not stood up to her family and fought harder for her baby.

So many reasons, so many excuses, but the truth was she had not trusted God to reach in and let Derrick understand her actions.

Ellie had lived with regret, knowing she had deprived them all of the chance to be a family. She could not change the past, or the decisions she had made, but she could reach out and ask for peace. Ellie knew with an inner knowledge only God could give her that peace, and she knew she only had to ask to receive it. So she did.

Broken Clouds

Broken clouds
Broken toy
Broken shoe
Broken car
Broken vow
Broken love
Broken heart
Broken life

And that is how she had felt: broken, not quite whole. Everything was there in her life—her family, her friends and her work—but still she had this feeling that something was not right within her.

Amanda glanced at the trees planted to hide manmade noise barriers; planted to hide the ugliness of unbroken concrete; planted to pretend the road wound through lush forest instead of breaking the continuity of suburban dwellings. Everything around her was false. Each time she drove under concrete and steel overpasses, built to connect one side of the motorway with the other, the lie of the trees was exposed.

During her quick sideways glance, Amanda realised that not everything was false. The flashes of yellow she saw amongst the green leaves she recognised as flowering mimosa—Australian wattle—and she smiled.

Spring; it must be spring, she thought. Then, in almost the same nanosecond, she realised they were still in the last month of winter and the trees had been fooled into flowering by the warmer than usual temperatures of the past winter.

'Typical,' Amanda muttered as a road sign, indicating it was time to merge with the left lane in preparation for crossing the bridge, caught and brought her attention back to her driving. 'Deception is all around and nothing is as it seems.'

The traffic lights turned from green to amber to red; Amber stopped, first in line for the next change, glanced right, then left, and checked her rear mirror before lifting her eyes to the bright blue sky littered with white, fluffy clouds. Waiting for the lights, but looking at the clouds drifting far above her, Amanda saw that they, also, were not as they seemed. The clouds were not a continuous whole entity but were breaking apart, shifting and changing in different ways by the air moving in the higher altitudes.

They were always moving, changing from shape to shape. First the head and wings of a beautiful angel drifted into the ears and inquisitive nose of a rabbit, or the trumpeting trunk and large ears of an elephant, or a startled duck with wings all aflap, then elongating out into a stallion riding the waves, until the shifting shape of the clouds eventually became an angel again.

Always moving, yet the clouds were ever really the same. Even when bits of the cloud broke away from the changing shapes to merge with other drifting wisps of cloud, creating new pictures, the cloud groups were fundamentally the same, always encouraging and enticing the eye to look closer, to look deeper to see what was hidden within its formation.

The lights changed and Amanda checked that her path was clear before leading the line of cars behind her onto the bridge. Amanda glanced at the water beneath the bridge, and saw that even though the clouds on high were playing a breeze, the water of the bay was millpond still.

With her new insight into how things were not as they seemed, Amanda realised that as beautifully reflective as the water was, there were probably life-and-death dramas being carried out in the depths of the ocean at that very moment. Again, here, right in front of her, was yet another example of how surface appearances were deceptive.

From her own perception of how things should be done, Amanda had lived her life in such a way that anyone seeing her, anyone talking to her, would think that she was 'doing okay' and was at peace with her lot in life. If anyone over the years had ever asked Amanda about her life, she would have probably never even recognised that she was hiding unsettled feelings and uneasy thoughts.

It had not been until a lady called Kelly was invited to speak at a ladies' meeting that Amanda had felt a pause in her heart. It had not been a big pause, and it had not hurt, but it had definitely been there—a small hiccup in the continuum that was her 'okay' life.

Kelly had experienced the traumatic life of a child from a broken home; then she was abused by a family friend; from that came an unwanted pregnancy, and then there was the pain of the decision she had been made to make. At the time, when Kelly shared her story, Amanda had thought, *That is really sad, and it is good that Kelly has been able to come through it all.*

But Kelly's story had not stopped there, in the pain of the past.

'I had not known that love could be soft, gentle, loving, peaceful, and something that should have made me feel secure. I had only known that love hurt and felt bad. Years later, I found myself sitting on the curb outside my home wondering whether life was worth living, when a gentleman wearing a long brown coat stopped and offered me his hand.

'It had been a very bad day in my life. I remember it was late and I thought, *Why is this man out at this time of night?* He didn't say anything; simply held out his hand to help me up from the gutter. I don't know why I accepted his hand but I did; he led me over to the bus seat on the side of the road. It was cold. I was cold, and he offered me his coat.

'He did not ask anything of me; he did not demand to know what was wrong. He just sat and let me be. And while we sat beside the road, on a cold, exposed wooden bus bench, warmth I had never known slowly slipped in around my heart, and I knew that I would be okay. I, used and abused as I was, was going to be okay because this quiet, gentle man just sat with me. I do not remember how long we sat there. I fell asleep, and when I awoke the man was gone, but I was warm because I was wrapped in a long brown coat.

'From that moment, I knew something had changed. Something had changed in me, and I knew I had to change some things in my life. I moved out of home, believing I could stand on my own two feet.

'It was difficult; I won't say it wasn't. I still was wary of people, didn't want people to become too close to me. I didn't want to open myself to being hurt or rejected again, but slowly I started playing a team sport, and sometime later a friend invited me to a meeting with her church ladies.

'I had never had much time for God, or the church, but I thought I had changed so much else in my life, so why not go with my friend to meet her friends. When I walked into the building it was strange, for it was like coming home. The place felt so warm and open that I didn't feel out of place.

'Then I saw him.

'He was standing at the far end of the room, looking at me.

'I recognised the warmth, love and acceptance on his face and I smiled.

'I was surprised to see him there. I wanted so badly to speak to the man again. I quickly told my friend I had seen someone I knew, then turned to walk over to talk to him, but he was gone.

'*Where has he gone*, I thought, and started to look around. My friend asked what the matter was, so I told her about that night in the gutter. I quickly followed up by telling her, "I saw him here, just a moment a go. But when I went to go to him he was gone."'

Kelly had paused, and Amanda had seen how the retelling of her story had brought a soft glow to Kelly's face. Amanda was amazed to feel the glow seemed to be reaching for her, so she closed her eyes and let it touch her world-weary heart. All too soon Kelly was again sharing her story. Amanda sat forward in her seat; she did not want to miss one single word.

'It appeared, however, that I was in the right place at the right time, because my friend seemed to understand my bewilderment. This was not the first time she had heard of the man who came to comfort the disheartened.

'My friend smiled at me, and then, taking my hand, we walked to a couple of empty chairs, where she said, "I think it best if we sit while I speak about the man I know. This man has a heart so big He is able to love everyone in the world, individually and as a whole. He is able to take a heart full of pain, and heal it with His compassion, understanding and acceptance. He paid the price required to receive forgiveness of all our sins. He came to prepare the way for God's Holy Spirit, who has come to guide us through the drama of life. He has at His command a multitude of angels. These He sends to comfort us in our times of hopeless darkness. His name is Jesus the Christ, Son of God, Saviour of the World, the personification of God's love on Earth."

'The more my friend talked, the more I knew it had been this man who had reached out to me. He had sent to me an angel in my time of brokenness, my time of hurt, to fill my heart with His love, warmth and hope, giving me His courage to change my life.

'Then my friend said something marvellous. She said that I could do the same for Him.

'Just as He had given His life as an invitation for me to know forgiveness and peace, I could invite Him into my life. All I had to do was believe He is the Son of God and, even though I could never deserve it, He came to die in my place. He came to give me the gift of love and life. I didn't have to promise great things, or do anything to win for Him.

'In fact, my friend told me that nothing I did would ever make Jesus love me more than He already does. Just as nothing I did would ever make Him love me less. And that was the amazing message for me, because all He wanted, all He asked, was that I love Him the same way.'

Kelly finished by saying that we could guess she did that—she invited Jesus into her life, into her heart—and wanted us all to know that we could do the same.

Kelly said, 'Jesus loves you and accepts you just as you are. You don't have to earn His love. You don't have to do anything for Him to love you, He already does. All He asks is for you to love Him in return.'

At that moment, Amanda thought, *Wow, in my own way I too have felt broken and not whole, like something was missing and I have worked to make it okay. Is it really so easy—am I already acceptable to God? I have tried so hard to make myself worthy and still didn't know if I had made it. Now here is Kelly telling me that all I have to do is to love Jesus and let Him love me. Is it really that simple?*

At that very moment, Amanda heard a small voice say to her, 'Yes, will you do it?'

Amanda found she could do nothing else but answer, 'Yes.'

Over the following weeks, Amanda's heart sang with the joy of living. Not a joy where she laughed out loud, even though she did do that too, no, her new joy was one of peace and love. This joy was one where she often found herself smiling at nothing at all. Something inside had shifted and, just like the clouds, her life had been reshaped, reformed, renewed with a feeling of hope. No longer would all the broken bits of her life be hiding in little boxes, Amanda had discovered, the more she trusted Jesus to continue to make all her broken bites whole, the more honest she was with everyone. Just as Jesus accepted her, in her own way, she was giving other people the opportunity to know and accept her, with all her faults, just as she was learning to accept them.

Amanda now believed that everyone has a plan at birth, but then life happens, and with every situation they face the plan for their lives adapts and re-forms. And as it happened with Amanda, with every re-forming there were little bits breaking off, little bits of hurt and disappointment, which were put away so that they were not thought of. But people just like Amanda were never quite the same after storing bits of pain in the little boxes of their hearts and minds.

And, like Amanda, they put on an I-am-doing-just-fine-thank-you-for-asking face. They forgot there was ever a time when they did not hide parts of themselves, because they were afraid of being hurt and rejected.

Amanda wanted all her family, and friends, to have what she had received, so she prayed and asked Jesus for this. But instead of answering Amanda in the way she expected, Jesus opened her 'compassionate eyes' so she was able to see that other people were also like the clouds. And as such, needed to answer 'Yes' for themselves: she, Amanda, could not answer for them.

Amanda could see that until her family and friends allowed Jesus to bring all their broken pieces together and make them whole, they would continue to live life a little bit broken. Until that time, they would continue to be like the clouds Amanda loved to watch. They would be shaped, and reshaped, by the events in their lives. They would continue to hide little boxes of pain, showing people just a side of themselves, but not really ever allowing anyone to see the whole picture.

Driving to work was now a time when Amanda was able to pray to Jesus to open the hearts of her family and friends so that they would recognise the voice of Jesus, and have the courage to say 'Yes' to His question.

You Can't Drive Two Cars at Once

Recently I had an accident on the motorway. Well, to be truthful, I was the 'tail-end Charlie' in a four-car pile-up. Thanking the Lord that the other cars all drove away with minimum damage to themselves or their people. While I, with considerable damage to my pride, stood by listening to the tow-truck driver give his considered opinion on the chances of my car ever being driven again. *Probably totalled,* were the words he used to describe its condition.

Days went by, my wishful hopes went toward a 'write-off', because thoughts of new-car shopping was to me, of course, exciting. However, new-car shopping turned out not to be on the agenda as my car was, in fact, miraculously repaired without a great deal of trouble to me.

I drive with a great deal of consideration and traffic awareness.

It is true, I do!

What was that comment?

Did I hear you say, 'Prove it?'

Well, I suppose the only real recommendation of my driving would have to come from someone I have not bumped into.

The simple fact that I have made four insurance claims since moving to the city four years ago is no indication of how careful I usually am on the road. However, after this last incident I have given my driving skills quite a bit of thought, and can only assume the monstrous four-wheel drive was using an alien cloaking device because I am sure it was not visible until I hit it.

When I rerun the incident and think of the size of vehicle I bumped, I have to ask myself, *Where was my concentration?*

And I am sure you will agree, once you realise that these new SUVs' high-viz transporters are made to stand out, with taillights up, and down, on every surface on the rear of the vehicle. At times, it seems my own small sedan is constantly being overshadowed by wannabe bush bashers. Maybe even bullied into believing there is no place left on the roads, for it or its own kind.

It is because I am so aware of these monsters taking over the roadways that I am as puzzled as ever as to how I did not see its glaringly bright eyes flashing, telling me to stop. One thing I do know, and that is that I am now very conscious of the stopping distance between my dear little green car and other cars travelling with me.

I give extra time at roundabouts, traffic lights and when crossing lanes to enable me to safely continue my journey. Probably to the irritation of everyone else on the road, but hey, I have heard it said that it is better to be safe than sorry.

The thing is that even with all of this extra care I take on the road, I cannot, in all honesty, say the way I drive now feels any different to the way I had been driving before my accidental meeting with the huge four-wheel drive on the motorway.

Today, while travelling to work, I took particular notice of the traffic travelling in the same direction as myself. I saw vehicles of all sizes moving from lane to lane, passing each other, all with purpose, all knowing the best way to arrive at their destination, in the best time they could. I saw some vehicles slow down to let others enter the lane in front of them; some came from nowhere and zoomed past me in an effort to save time, racing to be first to the traffic lights, like stallions on a raceway trying to prove they are the best of the mob. Some drivers seemed to be content to travel the road with a smile on their faces, knowing they were on time and had plenty of time to complete their journey. These drivers seemed to be oblivious to the frantic efforts of their fellow travellers zipping around them in the hope of pushing the contented drivers to join their race.

I remembered how, over the years, friends had shared their techniques on how they encouraged cars in front of them to hurry up when they, the friends, thought that they, the contented drivers, were not doing it right. By 'it', of course they meant that the other people were not driving fast enough, or passing quickly enough, or even just pulling over to the side of the road so that my friends could get past and be on their way.

Even as I remembered some of the very sound advice I had received, I smiled to see a driver of a Queensland-registered utility use the well-used tactic of crowding the car in front to make the driver increase their speed, or better still, force the car to change lanes by intimidating it.

While all these thoughts ran through my head, something I already knew became very clear in my thoughts. I realised that it really did not matter how close the utility drove to the car in front of it; the utility itself could not make people in the car in front of it drive any differently than they already were. The driver of the utility could not think the driver of the car into changing lanes, or accelerate uphill so that the utility could pass the car. The only way to actually determine how the car in front of the utility was driven was for the driver of the utility to drive the car as well.

Suddenly 'boof', like a lightning bolt, I got it.

I, too, can only drive one car at a time; therefore I can only be responsible for the speed and safety of my own vehicle. It still did not open up any brilliant insight into why I ran up the back of a fairly large-sized four-wheel drive, but still, it was a revelation to realise that only I could be responsible for my own vehicle and could not make other people drive in the way that I wanted them too.

Oh, I know: you knew this little titbit of information, and I suppose I did too, but it was the first time I had probably ever really admitted it.

As I watched the traffic around me, I did wonder how I could impart this brilliant revelation to my children, because of course I wanted them to benefit from my wisdom. After all, what is Mother for but to impart her wisdom and experience to her children? I mean to say, how are they ever going to learn if I do not tell them, show them and explain to them? And I certainly want them to learn a lesson about how to not crash their cars into large four-wheel-drive SUVs on the motorway. I wanted to tell them that no matter how much they zigzagged through the lanes or crowded the car in front of them, they would not get to their destination any faster, because wherever they went the traffic travelling with them would help to determine the speed they drove. That is, of course, unless they actually found a way to drive all the cars on the road with them all at once.

With a cautious eye and careful consideration of cars flowing around me, I continued to drive to work, slowed down for road works, indicated when I needed to change lanes, stopped at traffic lights, and followed all the rules of the road. All the while my thoughts were flying along the multitude of times where I had tried to drive another person's car as well as my own.

My children were a perfect example. I could not help thinking how I guided them through childhood by instructing them on a multitude of everyday tasks. Like how to mow the lawn; how to wash the dishes; how to study; how to do assignments; how to talk to people; how to make friends; how to practise and play sport; how to light a fire; how to boil a kettle; how to make a bed, clean a room, and wash the car. The list was endless; each time I would show them how to do the task I would sit back and mentally go through each step of the task with them just to make sure that they did it the *right* way.

You guessed it: *my right way.*

I admit there were times when I lost my cool over them not 'doing it right', then I would get in there and give them the benefit of my expertise by showing them again, and, if needed, yet again.

I remember there were many times when I had been determined to drive their car for them, for each and every task, journey.

Even when I finally got the message—through not only my own parents, but parenting groups, teachers, even at times scout leaders—that my children had to do the tasks themselves and find a way that worked best for them, I still tried to drive their car. I was so determined to make sure that the way they tackled each task throughout their life would still be *my way*.

Yes, you can laugh. You have probably never gone in after your children have 'helped' you and 'fixed' things up. I imagine that you have never gone back and rewashed the dishes, or re-mowed the lawn so that it was 'just so', or gone out to rehang the washing because the underwear was on the outside of the line.

Driving off the bridge—no, you are wrong, I am not driving into the water to end my thought pattern but simply exiting the bridge, via the road, with the other cars—and winding my way around the beach road to my place of work, my thoughts moved on to how I had also been trying to drive my children's spiritual growth.

When I first became involved with church life, I went to everything that was on. It was great: I developed a great relationship with Jesus, I met new friends, and I just loved to share my new life with everyone. If I thought about my children at all, I would have thought that because I was getting so much out of the meetings, they would be too. I admit I did not give much thought to them needing to drive their own car, drive their own walk of faith.

Until now I had not given any thought to the actual fact that it did not matter what I did, or what I said, or to how many prayer nights or conferences I took them too—it was their walk and it would never be the same as mine. I could take them to all the meetings I wanted to, but at the end of the day I could not make them receive the same message as me. The words we heard would be the same, but the meaning we gave to them would be different because, simply, we had different understandings of what the words meant in our lives.

That was a hard one to grasp, but then came the next step in my revelation.

I was suddenly aware of all the people I wanted to know the same faith walk that I was enjoying. They crowded my mind and filled my thoughts, and I knew I would never be the same again, because I could tell them, and I could share with them everything I knew, but they would never really 'get it' like me, simply because they were not me, and they never would be. That did not mean that they would not have their own faith in God, or their own understanding of who Jesus is and what He did for them on the cross at Calvary; it just meant that I could not 'drive their car' for them.

No matter how much I wanted to help them grow in their trust and faith in God, there was absolutely nothing I could do but pray for the Grace of God to show them how much they meant to God.

Why not, was not even a question I needed to ask myself because it seemed nearly too simple. We are all different; we have had different life experiences, and we view the world differently because of them. We all have different needs, and God meets all our needs, which means we all meet the part of God we need at the time we need Him.

With the Pacific Ocean on one side of me and low suburbia on the other, I was hit with another realisation; and that was, it is okay for others to have different thoughts and feelings about Christianity. It's very okay for people to have a different faith walk and to make different choices, because God did not make us all the same to be the same in all ways. He made us to challenge the choices that we made; He made us to talk about our differences, and these very differences helped us through our tough times.

'Judge not or yea shall be judged' is not exactly a quote from the Bible, but close enough to be a constant reminder to me to be kind to people. I realised that it was very easy for me to look at other people,—my children included—and think that because they were not like me, not behaving like me, then they were missing something.

Even as these thoughts filled my mind, I was convinced in my heart that my children and other people were driving their cars in the best way that they could. It was not for me to judge what they did or did not know. I was not to judge because others were behaving differently to me, but rather I was to love them, and accept them for who they were, leaving their choices and heart issues for God to take care of.

Why it has taken me so many years to 'get' this foundational teaching, I do not know. All I know is that it is real and it is true. I cannot *make* anyone else make the same choices as me.

So, like driving on a shared motorway, I need to tend to my own car, walk my own journey and be responsible for myself. Just like I cannot drive two cars at once on the highway, it is impossible for me to walk someone else's life path; I cannot *make them* find peace and loving acceptance in Jesus. I can only share the knowledge and faith experience I have, and pray that their ears and hearts are open to receiving the Good News message that is: Jesus came, He died for us and He lives still, wanting us to ask Him into our lives.

Reversing competently into a handy parking space alongside my place of work, I thanked God for His wisdom when, in my own ignorance, He had given me the words to encourage friends and family not to judge their children, or their partners, just because they made different decisions and choices.

With my hand on the door handle and ready to start work, I was reminded that the lesson of 'only being able to control my own journey' was not really a new one. Thinking on this for a moment, I could remember opportunities when I had encouraged young people in the church to have their own faith in God and not just give Him an imitation of their parents' faith. He wanted their own faith; these were times I had been encouraging them to drive their own cars.

Since I have had the car repaired, people have asked me how I am, how is the car, what happened. The answers I have are: I am good; my car is repaired; and the why is in the past and does not need to be hashed over.

I still do not know how I managed to be in the accident, but I do know that out of my incident with a four-wheel-drive car I have an identifiable image to be able to encourage others to drive their own car. I know to ask God to be the driver with me, and to keep me awake and aware while on the road. I appreciate God's protection over myself, my car, and other people on the road with me. So, Godspeed to all of you who drive, may you also be awake and aware for the whole of your journey.

So Many Flowers

So many flowers, so many cards and so many people, yet not one of them the person he needed to see. Not one of them the person he would never see again.

An audible sigh rose from the pain in his heart, and Ben gave voice to his fears. 'What am I going to do without you?'

It had been so quick. True, Julie had not been feeling well for a couple of weeks, but that could have been the 'flu shot they had both had back in January. Then, at the beginning of March, there was a bout of the sniffles that never went away; everyone seemed to have it, so Julie had not been worried. Then she had been diagnosed with cancer.

The doctors said that with treatment, her percentages of survival would be greatly increased. It was true that no one had actually hinted there could be a complete recovery, or even a long-term remission of Julie's cancer. Still, what could they do but take the slim chance that they would have more time together.

So she had started the chemotherapy. It did not matter how much Ben had tried to be a part of her sickness, or her treatment, the truth was, at the end of the day, if he wanted to, he could walk away for a few minutes, or a few hours, and his life would still go on. He had been, and still was, guilt ridden because he could always have a break, while Julie lived with cancer cells multiplying faster than her normal healthy cells.

It had been so surreal to sit in those comfortable blue chairs, with soft music playing, coffee on offer, even a cream biscuit if he had wanted, and have people at the cancer place explain so simply that cancer cells were just malformed cells. They were an aberration of the normal way cells grew and rested.

Ben had never given any thought as to how the human cell reproduced itself. It was just something that happened. He had never thought about cells having a memory of what the organ, it belonged to should be like. It was not something he used as part of his daily conversation, or thought pattern. No one he knew had ever asked him whether or not an individual cell knew what it should look like, or knew how it should function to enable the human body to work and renew itself.

He had never before thought about how, once new cells replaced worn-out ones, they stopped and rested until it was time for them, in turn, to be replaced. It had been a wonder for him to hear how there were only ever a certain amount of cells needed to make up each individual part of the human body, and how only worn-out ones were ever replaced.

He learnt that the human body never made more cells than those needed for an organ to do its job. The thing with a cancer cell, he discovered, was that it did not have this ingrained information to rest, to stop multiplying itself. It amazed him to learn cancer cells were so dangerous because they continued to reproduce, continued to multiply twenty-four hours a day; they never rested.

Why am I even thinking about this now?

Ben remembered it was much better to fill his mind with anything rather than thinking about Julie. His heart, lying in the beautifully decorated casket lined with pale blue satin, waiting to be placed in the ground. He did not want to think about her there, in her final resting place. He did not want to think that after, after ... He did not want to think that he would then be leaving her there, surrounded by family and friends who had gone on before to that 'better place'.

He had already chosen her headstone. Well, Julie had insisted on going with him to choose it. She had wanted to be a part of the whole process. She planned her funeral service and the songs to be sung.

She even wrote a note to give everyone who came to say goodbye. That was his Julie, thinking of how to make it easier for everyone around her.

Putting his head in his hands, Ben's whole body shook with anguish of his heart. Mentally, he cried out in the hope there would be an answer.

What am I going to do now?

Who will laugh with me? Who will share my morning cuppa?

Who will tease me when I 'cheat' while doing the crossword puzzle?

Who will listen to my words, but not my heart?

Who will ... oh God, there are so many who-wills mingling with all the what-ifs, why-nows and why-hers.

He knew he was sinking into that place where hope was hard to see, but he could not stop thinking, *What will I do? What can I do now that my best friend has gone from my life?*

Ben had no idea he was not alone until he was startled by the door closing with a 'bang'. Turning in his seat to enable him to see who had entered the room, he was surprised to find a small boy. Guilt was written all over the boy's face. Another giveaway that it was the boy who had allowed the door to slam was the hand he had held up to his mouth, as if to say, 'Oh no, I am in for it now.' Ben looked from the boy back to the casket at the front of the room. He was not ready yet to focus on something that looked like living.

The boy, after letting his bright blue eyes look around the room, realising that he had got away with letting the door bang, walked further into the room. It was just like the one he had come from. *Boring*, he thought. Not used to being quiet for very long, he looked at the grey-headed man he had spotted from the doorway. The man was sitting in the middle of the front row of maroon chairs, facing the front of the room. The boy quickly hopped, on both feet, over to where the man sat. The man did not look at him, so he sat down two chairs away and waited. But then he heard the door being opened, and he reached out and tugged on the sleeve of the man's jacket, saying, 'Oh mister, please could you not say that it was me who slammed the door?'

Just at that moment a stressed-looking young woman walked quickly through the door, crossed the room and said, 'I am so sorry, I hope Johnny is not bothering you; I only looked away for a moment, then he was gone.'

'Not at all,' the man replied. 'I hardly knew he was here.'

This answer immediately gave young Johnny the opportunity to pipe in. 'See, Mum, no trouble at all.' Then, turning to the grey man, he asked, 'If is all right with the man, Mum, can I stay a while.? Pleeeease, Mum. I'll be good. It's just …'

Johnny's mum, knowing what 'it's just' meant to

her son, turned her attention to the man, dressed in a good-quality three-piece dove-grey suit, and asked if her son could stay awhile.

Ben had been just sitting, waiting quietly with his wife for her service to begin. He shrugged and said, 'Sure, why not.' Ben introduced himself to Johnny's mum, and then listened while Johnny was given 'be good, I am not far away' instructions. Without saying anything more, Johnny's mum turned and walked out the way she had entered. Ben was aware she may have appeared to trust her son to a stranger, but she had left him the message 'I will be watching' by leaving the door ajar so she could keep an eye on her son.

Johnny sat down next to Ben. He was silent for all of two whole seconds while he looked at the room full of flowers. Then, because he could not help himself, Johnny blurted out all the words in his head. 'Boy, whoever got those flowers sure must have been loved. Look at all the pretty colours. I like the yellow ones best. Do you like the yellow ones, too?'

Without even waiting for a reply, Johnny jumped off his chair, hopped over to Julie's flowers and picked up a card, with a puppy dog in a field full of flowers on it, then slowly read it out. *Dear Ben, we are sorry for your loss. Julie was a great person and we loved her dearly.*

Again, without even stopping for a reply, Johnny

picked up another card with soft white ribbons with flowers etched in pink on it, and read aloud. *Dear Ben, we know that there is nothing anyone can say that will ease your pain, but Julie is now in a better place and at peace. May the Lord bless her and reach out His healing hand to you, and bring you peace.*

Johnny looked at the man and asked, 'Are you Ben?'

When the man replied saying he was, Johnny immediately followed with, 'Where is the better place that Julie went to? Are you in pain? Do you need to be healed? Are you sick?

'My little sister was sick but she died and went to Heaven.

'Is that where your Julie went too? I heard people say that Heaven was a better place.

'Will she see my little sister? If she does, do you think that she will play with her in the sandpits of Heaven?

'I was very sad when my little sister died, because I was afraid that she would have no one to talk to, no one to play with, and no one to hold her when she is scared. And she gets scared, 'specially if she sees a spider or something like that. I used to look after her, but I didn't know who would look after her in Heaven.

'I asked my mum if I could go to Heaven too, to be with my little sister, but she said no. I had to stay here with her. She said she didn't know how she would survive if we both went away. But if your Julie went to Heaven, then my little sister will have someone to talk to. Your Julie looks nice, and she looks like she would be kind to my sister. I am really sorry that you lost your Julie, but it makes me happy to know that she might be with my sister.'

Ben stood up, walked over to stand beside the beautiful flowers, and picked up Julie's picture. He indicated that Johnny should give him the card, and then squatted on the floor beside him. They were both silent while they looked at Julie's smiling face. Ben remembered the day the photo had been taken, and Julie's smile; it was another thing to miss. Exhaling his resignation, Ben said, 'Yes, Johnny, my Julie has gone to Heaven. She was very sick, and after having lots of medicine she went to Heaven to be with our Lord Jesus.

'Heaven is known as "a better place" by people because it is a place where there is no pain; there is only love and laughter all day long. I have been very sad because I, too, did not want her to go without me. But she also said I could not go with her. I had to stay here.

'I am a little like your mother; I do not know how I am going to survive without her.'

Johnny reached out his little hand and laid it on Ben's hand, then leaned his head against Ben's arm.

The act of acknowledging pain and all the sincerity of an innocent heart touched Ben, and he thought, *There is so much sadness in the world, and I have been so focused on me and what will I do that I have forgotten I am not the only one in pain.*

Ben patted Johnny's shoulder in thanks before continuing. 'Johnny, you are a very wise young man, because listening to you has reminded me that I, too, have children who need me to be here with them. I have friends who are missing my Julie just as much as I am, and they need me as much as I need them.

'You, young man, have shown me, with your words that I needed Jesus to show me that it was all right for Julie to go to Heaven without me. In my sadness, I had forgotten that Jesus wants to share this part of my life as well as all the happy times. I had forgotten that Jesus will hold me tight when I am sad and missing her. I had forgotten He does this because He loves me. And he loves you and your mummy, too.'

Ben stood up and picked up one of the sympathy cards before leading Johnny back to the maroon chair; he was, after all, no longer a young man like his new friend. Once seated, Ben wanted to encourage Johnny to continue to believe that his sister had someone to play with.

'Johnny, I want you to have faith and trust that Jesus is with your sister, and with my Julie. They are not alone, and they will have someone to talk to, and someone to play with while they wait for us to live our lives, here on earth.

'I am sorry your little sister died.

'Thank you for telling me about her, because I think you are right, and my Julie will love playing with her in Heaven.

'Johnny, I had been very sad and I had been asking Jesus to show me how to live without my Julie. And, Johnny, I believe Jesus sent you to me, to tell me about your sister, and your mummy, and so that He, Jesus, could tell me to keep on living here, and loving Him.'

Ben felt he needed to give Johnny due respect for the wisdom he had given, so he formally took Johnny's little hand and shook it in a man's handshake. 'Johnny, I know that even as you miss your sister and I miss my Julie, Jesus will always be with you and your mummy. When the pain in your heart gets too big, I would like you to remember to call out for Jesus to come and help you. And I know He will, because He loves you and He is with you, always.

'To help you remember both Julie and I, as well as Jesus' love for you, I would like you to take this card with you.'

'Oh no, Ben, my mum will think that I just took it.'

'I will explain that I gave it to you, that is, if you would like it.'

'Oh, yes please, if you don't mind.'

Johnny looked at the card covered in yellow-and-blue flowers his new friend had given him.

Inside, the words read: *Dear Ben, there are times when we just do not know why something happens. And going to Heaven at such an early age is one of these times. At these times we question ourselves and God. I want to encourage you, even in your pain, to ask Jesus to reach out His healing hand and touch your hurting heart, so that the pain of your loss will never be too much to bear. Your pain is His pain and He will bring you peace because He loves you. So, Ben, I urge you to find the time to be still, and let Jesus save you from your despair. Love always, Julie.*

Ben replaced Julie's picture amongst the fragrant flowers and sympathy cards, then he asked, 'If it is all right with you, I would like to walk with you to find your mother. Then we will be able to explain about the card.' Johnny nodded his head and reached up to take Ben's hand.

Leaving the room with Johnny, Ben was glad it was time for him to start sharing the peace now filling his heart with others. It was time to celebrate the life he had shared with Julie, as his wife. He knew his grief would not suddenly disappear just because he had been reminded others were missing Julie too.

Ben accepted that it would not always be easy

to live without Julie. He accepted there would be times when he would hit rock bottom without her. Talking to Johnny, and remembering Julie telling him he could not go with her, had brought about this acceptance in his heart. Ben left the room with a glimmer of hope in his heart. He was not completely alone; there were people who needed him, even as he needed them.

Ben knew it had not been talking to Johnny that had worked peace into his heart. All the thanks had to go to *the only One who is able* to heal a hurting heart. In giving thanks to Jesus, Ben's heart, and head, acknowledged that it was time to release Julie to God, and walk in the freedom of knowing that one day they would be together again.

One Day a Raindrop Fell

One day a little raindrop fell. He did not know that he was a raindrop at the time. No, he had been warm and safe, filled with love and life, surrounded by fun and friends.

He existed in a place where time did not exist; where he was never hungry or cold; where he was never sick or upset. He just knew that he was alive, and he was happy to be where he was.

Then, one day, things in his world were different.

If he were asked what the difference was, he would not have been able to say what was different. He could not have even pinpointed the time when things around him changed. One moment everything was the same, and then suddenly all those around him were whispering and crowding together to bump off each other. An inner excitement grew bigger and bigger as he too was bumped, tossed and rumbled around with everyone else.

Something bright slashed across the sky, startling him.

Then he heard it: a very, very, very loud sound. He heard a voice laugh and call out its 'thunder'. He was surprised to discover the voice was his, because behind the laughter he heard a hint of fear.

Without warning he was being rushed out of his warm, happy place into a big open area surrounded by dark, heavy-looking clouds that made him frown. It was different from before; for a moment he saw the difference around him; he saw a difference in him and realised that he was a little scared of what was happening to his world.

Just as suddenly as the fear appeared, it disappeared, and he was happy. No, it was more than that: he was overjoyed to be tumbling, racing, and falling with everyone else toward the earth.

How did he know that he was falling?

He did not; all he knew was that he was no longer where he used to be and movement was all around him.

Previously, he had just been where he was and, if he thought about being somewhere else, he was. He had not gone up, or down, or moved sideways. Before the thunder, he had just existed and it had been good.

But now it was different. Now, for the first time in his life, he was listening to others talking and laughing around him.

He had never needed to talk before, but now he was full of words and laughter. They were words he had not heard before, yet he knew what the words meant. He understood what others were saying, calling out, yelling at each other, and he too was talking, yelling out and laughing.

He could not have known that he and the others were welcome on the earth. He could not have known that the people who lived on the earth had been praying for rain. They had been calling out to God. Asking for rain to pour out of the storm clouds they had seen growing on the horizon. They wanted it to rain because the land was dry and the crops would not grow without it.

The little raindrop could not have known that people living on the land celebrated, with great joy, when rain fell from the sky. For, after all, he was only a little raindrop and what did he know of life on the land?

Suddenly he was free of the dark clouds and he laughed with joy each time he bounced off the other raindrops as they plunged towards the earth. None of the raindrops knew what was happening to them, or where they would end up. They could not know that some of them would land on the tops of buildings and end up in big plastic tanks. The tanks had been set up by the people to collect the rain whenever it fell from the sky and landed on their rooftops.

The raindrops could not know that some of them would end up on the dry land to simply disappear into wide cracks dissecting the thirsty land. They could not know that some of them would fall into the ocean and be absorbed into that vast expanse of water, to live as though they had never existed as individual raindrops. They would arrive full of life and expectation, only to discover that they were not special; in fact, they were no different from the other drops of water in the ocean. They would forget that they were meant to laugh and share the joy of their life with others.

The raindrops could not know that some of them would land on the tips of tall trees, run down a leaf, and then complete their downward journey by landing with a splash in a small trickle of water. A small trickle that wound around granite boulders buried deep between the trees. They could not know the small trickle would follow a predestined path down the mountainside to pool in a small rocky gully. These raindrops could not know that other trickles would join them in the pool, which would then overflow its boundaries and lead them into a wondrous adventure as they travelled toward the ocean.

All the raindrop knew was that he felt he had been lucky to land on the tip of a tall tree—and so began his journey to the sea. He raced with the best of them, bouncing around granite boulders and jumping over little twigs carelessly hidden in the grass. The freshness and the power of raindrops racing together moved some of them to shout, and laugh out loud, when they realised they were not alone in their race to reach the bottom of the mountain.

The raindrop laughed and sang of his joy with the rest of them.

He called to the trees, telling them of his joy and of all the wondrous things he saw. He told them about the slippery green moss growing on the sides of rocks, barely covered by stagnant water, in small pools around the gully floor. The moss, too, was happy to be blanketed under the rush of water formed by the raindrops. For the moss had also been waiting for the rain to bring new life to their pools, so that it too could play its part in the cycle of life as it became food for the frogs and fish that lived in the pools.

It had been a long time since the last rain had fallen in the mountains, and everything had been calling out to the heavens for fresh, sweet rain. Everything had been waiting for the power of the new water to force its way into the gullies; pushing and pulling all the stones and rocks around so the small pools were washed clean of rotting leaves and stale water.

The little raindrop sang out to tell the trees he could see the little fish hiding between their roots. This was nothing new to the trees, for they knew that their long roots, breaking through hard-packed dirt reaching for the last of the water, were a place of refuge for the little fish while everyone waited on the life-bringing rain. All the little fishes peeped out, knowing the fresh water would bring fresh food even as it brought a deadly danger. They knew that if they did not secure themselves beneath the trees' roots the roar of the fresh life could flush them out and carry them miles from their home

The little raindrop did not know how powerful or dangerous his boisterous race could be to those who were used to a quieter way of living. Even the solidly rooted trees gripped more tightly and tried to slow his pace by warning him about large rocks that rose up from out of the riverbed.

'They will launch you high into the air in an effort to diffuse your enthusiasm; for the rocks will separate you from your friends and scatter them all in different directions.'

The little raindrop laughed at the trees' warning, telling the trees he was not afraid because he had tackled rocks before. He told how he had raced right up to the rocks, ridden up the side of them, and jumped right over their heads. He told them how he had landed with a splash, and a laugh, on the other side of them, and then he had hurried to continue in the race to be first.

At that moment nothing seemed to be too hard for the little raindrop, because while he raced with the others he felt invincible. When he came to the rocks the trees had warned him about, he noticed that not every raindrop survived the jump and the splash as he did. Some flew high and landed on the grassy sides of the waterway, and ended their race by slipping down a dry stalk of grass to become one with the earth; some landed with a crash on a rock and broke into pieces, becoming mist rising high into the air only to be absorbed by moisture-hungry leaves. But the raindrop had little time to think on another's journey for he was being rushed onward.

With the other raindrops, he talked and laughed so loudly people in the fields could hear him before they ever saw him. He felt wonderful; he felt powerful; he felt like he could move mountains, and in truth, as long as he rushed along with the others, he was part of a force that could indeed move mountains. For wherever he went, the energy he was part of changed everything it touched; he was part of living water flowing from the heavens.

All during his headlong rush down through the mountains, over rocky rapids, he was filled with excitement and he pushed to be first. Even though he did not really understand where they were going, he wanted to yell, 'Follow me; I know the way.' He felt he knew everything there was to know and so was confident that he really could lead the way.

But he did not really know everything; his own exuberance fed him as he raced with the other raindrops. On and on they surged until they ran out of mountain, and each drop separated as it was flung far out into a void. The little raindrop forgot about his friends and the race to be first, for he felt he could fly. Far out into the void he flew, then, with the rest of his companions, he fell a great distance and sank into the wide, still pool at the bottom of a waterfall.

The little raindrop had been quite frightened at the time; to suddenly stop and be still was disturbing. So he waited. Everything that had happened to him since he had left his soft warm place had been none of his doing, so he waited to see what would happen now.

He clung to the edges of the pool and he allowed his awareness to explore the stillness. After a time he became certain that there was a deception at work in the pool, hoping to cause the fear of the unknown in the hearts of little raindrops. He knew this because the more he listened to the stillness, and felt with his senses, the more he realised that there was a quiet, steady current gently moving the water forward. Softly calling, enticing, asking, pleading for him to come away from the edges of the pool and ride the current flowing from the pond into the river. The voice promised a never-ending life as it relentlessly headed towards the source of all rain: the wide-open oceans.

When he accepted the invitation to move forward, he discovered he was not alone; both new and old friends were moving with him. After a while of being comfortable and secure, the little raindrop became even a little bored with the slow, steady flow of the larger river. He began to miss the rush; the rough and tumble of the small stream.

In the stream he had felt filled with the purpose and power that came from a small stream moving at speed. So he asked himself while he moved steadily along, 'Am I actually going anywhere? Is this it for me, or is there a way out of this gently flowing river into a smaller, more exciting stream?'

He thought that maybe he was in the wrong river, for he heard there were other, bigger, more energetic rivers having loads of fun as they travelled their journey to the ocean. Even though he kept his thoughts to himself, it was not long before he heard drops of water around him whispering to each other that they were unhappy because they missed the excitement of their first stream.

He was not one to grumble or join in when others grumbled, so he kept to himself and gave himself some time to see what this river had around its bends. While he waited, some of the grumblers edged over to the sides of the river and allowed themselves to be diverted to feeder-flows in the hope of finding what they thought they had lost. The little raindrop saw them go and hoped they would fare well, but he was not inclined to rush after them.

After a while he realised he had, unknowingly, become inwardly excited about being in the wide, deep river as it carried him relentlessly, strongly, through the thirsty, dry land. He realised it was a different kind of joy, a different kind of excitement from before. He no longer wanted to shout aloud with joy because he had a sense of peace, a sense of contentment within himself.

He thought, *Yes, I enjoyed the boisterous stream when I had raced and laughed out loud, but the wide depth of the river gives me a sense of life-changing purpose when I flow past strong, tall trees standing by the water. I have a sense of being part of something bigger than myself.* With startling, sudden insight he knew that he was just one little raindrop, but he made a difference. Without him, the river would still flow but it would be down the energy, the power and the excitement of one more raindrop. He was very happy to be the extra energy and power the river needed to make its impact on the land.

While the river flowed strongly onward, he had a chance to look around, see the world, and learn a little about the life on the land. He could see broken-down homesteads where people no longer lived because there had been no rain, and the water had dried up. He saw the danger of fallen, dead gum trees, fallen because the rain had not come, and grass that held the dirt of the banks had died. The little raindrop looked and wondered, *Did the soil break away because the grass died, or did the great big grey trees fall because the ground they grew in wasn't solid enough?*

He did not know, but he looked and he learnt that water created by individual raindrops, moving together, healed and helped the land, and the people, to survive. He saw townspeople standing on the riverbanks and bridges watching in wonder as the water swirled by. He saw animals with their heads down peacefully eating grass that was already growing on the banks of the river. At one time he was nearly jumped on by a small person swinging out of a tree, landing with a splash in the water, laughing with his human friends.

The little raindrop, because he was water, could not really understand just how important he was to the land and the people, and so casually lay on his back and looked at the stars. He did not need to carry the responsibility of moving mountains or bringing life to the land; he just had to enjoy his journey. And, at that moment, for him enjoyment was to roll onto his back and look at the wonder of the star-filled night sky. Floating along and looking up, he let the peace and strength of the river seep into him.

Just when he thought there would be nothing more to his journey than the peace and comfort of the river, he heard shouts of laughter ahead of him. Even though he could not understand what was being shouted, he suddenly stopped moving forward and was thrown high into the air to fall back with a splash. Something wondrous had happened; he had never heard the expression 'where the river meets the sea', but that was what was happening. His river had met the sea and everything in his life was changing again.

No longer was the river moving steadily forward, but it was clashing with the incoming tide as it fought to reach the open water of the ocean. No longer was he safe and secure in a calm place, but he was once again being urged on to surge forward, urged to renew his desire to be first in the race. Only now it was a race to tell the raindrops that had fallen into the ocean about the wonders of bringing life to the land.

Instead of being scared of the change in pace, he was suddenly awake and excited again.

Just when he thought that there would be nothing else in his life, he was in the middle of a tidal, tugging current and fighting madly to be first to join with the ocean waters. The little raindrop wondered now, as he fought to break through the salt-heavy drops of water, how he had ever thought there was nothing else to do but reach the ocean, reach the end of his journey.

He knew he was up to the battle to reach the ocean; he knew he was strong enough because he had been a part of the wide, deep, flowing river. It had been a long time since he had realised that slow and steady had not meant weak. The raindrops forming the river may have been silent while they flowed strongly together to clear away sandbanks, shift big granite rocks from the riverbed, and remove fallen trees from the riverbanks, but they had not lost their voices. The channel rang with laughter and shouts of victory as the raindrops raced to be the first again.

During his experiences, from the sky to the ocean, the little raindrop had discovered his journey was not just about him having fun and doing exciting things all the time. No, he had learnt how powerful his river became when the other little raindrops joined together with one purpose, and travelled in one direction. He had learnt how important it was to stop and listen to the softly whispering voice of the strong, wide, deep river. If he had not answered the call to 'come', then he would never have left the safe, calm place in the pool at the bottom of the waterfall. He would never have known the wonder of changing lives by bringing life-giving water to dry souls. He would never have had the opportunity to make a difference to the environment because he was part of something so much more powerful than himself.

Not all the raindrops had been as lucky as he had been. Some had fallen into the ocean and had not had the chance to learn the things he had learned. They had not seen the things he had seen. He realised, as he rushed forward to meet the next surge of salty water that he wanted to tell them about the things he had seen and done. But, more than that, he wanted to hear about the things they had seen and done in the ocean.

The raindrop laughed out loud. *How wondrous this journey has been, and it is not over yet.*

What Lydia Knew

For Walter Leslie and Deidre Joy – thank you for giving me the opportunity to know what Lydia knew.

Kind-hearted people had been filling my every waking hour for the past three days, but this morning I had asked for solitude.

'I am as all right as I can be, but please let me have the morning,' I had pleaded with every kind voice. And surprisingly, they had.

I showered, dressed, and tidied the house. I even made a fresh pot of percolated coffee, and had it with hot buttered toast. I did all the things I usually did to start my day right, then I walked out the front door, forgetting both the coffee and the toast. And there they sit still, on my tidy kitchen counter. This morning my kitchen sink was not littered with plastic drink bottles or used glasses, the kitchen cupboard did not have grains of cereal and milk spilt on it; nothing was out of place, except for my toast and coffee cup.

My diary was equally tidy, with one appointment for the day. I insisted that I drive myself; after all, I had been driving for over twenty years. I arrived early and was greeted by an usher, who offered to show me to my place. I asked if it would be all right if I found it by myself. I knew there would be a lot of things that I would be doing by myself from now on. The silence of the building was neither welcoming nor uncomfortable; it was just silence.

I took my first step to the next phase of my life, and I could smell the beeswax that was used to preserve wood. The interior of the venue was beautifully serene. I could see the florist had given her best, and I could smell the gentle aroma of lavender in each of the purple bouquets I walked past. I looked toward the front of the room, knowing my place was down there, at the end of the aisle, and I saw the reason I was here. She would have loved it. Her place had been beautifully, gracefully arranged, with soft pink-and-purple materials draped around her picture. Multi-hued arrangements of pink-and-purple flowers filled the space around her. Yes, she would have loved it. It was only after I walked past the seats reserved for the bereaved to stand by my daughter that I allowed unanswerable questions to flood from my heart, and head.

Where do I start?
What is there to say?

Was there anything I could have done?

Was there ever anything to say … or do?

Some people say that from the moment we are born, our whole lives are already mapped out for us. Some say our end is a result of the choices we make. The Bible says, 'Only God knows the numbers of our days.' Sitting here, right now, in this place, I do not think it is fair; whatever the reasoning for ending her life, it is just not fair.

For myself, I would have forgone this ceremonial tribute, but my beautiful Lydia would have wanted to be in this place, where free will played an important part in the lives of men.

What happened to my free will?

I would have freely chosen to be sitting in an untidy kitchen with my daughter; I would definitely have chosen not to be here today.

So, if that was my free-will choice, whose had brought us here today?

Without even having to give any time to answering that particular question, I knew the answer … it was Lydia's. It was, of course, Lydia's choice to follow Jesus that had become the decision-maker that brought them to this place. I cannot help but wonder, *Is it because of Lydia's choice that I am here right now? I mean here, at this time?*

I had always planned to arrive early, because I wanted time to try to understand why my child was lying in a wooden casket. But I had definitely not needed to arrive nearly three-quarters of an hour before the service, or so I would have thought. Admittedly, it was a beautiful, beautiful casket; it was resting on a pedestal, in a room with a roof that arched its way a hundred feet above muted, multi-coloured marble tiles covering the floor.

The very size of the vaulted, wooden beams resting on solid stone columns, surrounded by multi-coloured lead-lined windows telling a story of love, ensured the building itself was enough to bring anyone to a place of silence and awe. This was a place where song rang out, where music resonated when the organist played, but this was not a place for casual comments, not a place where one came to gather, and share laughter. This was a place where marriages were blessed, babies were baptized, sins were confessed, farewells were said, and grace was received.

Is this it? Is this building the culmination of lives of loving, of giving? Is this all there is to life, birth, marriage, death, and all of it passing through buildings like this?

Lydia did not think so. Lydia believed there was so much more than a beautiful building.

Lydia had loved to come here, but she came to sit with Jesus, whenever she had a chance. I, on the other hand, had only come to appreciate the beautiful architecture, and the building's history of it. I had heard all the same stories and lessons read from the Bible, but I never understood Lydia's fascination with the 'who' of the first church.

One day Lydia had come home and talked about receiving the sacrificial, unconditional, enduring love of Jesus Christ. I had tried to understand what she was telling me, but I had been unable to comprehend a love like that. My experience with love had ended in disappointment and loneliness. And as though to reinforce my previous knowledge, my love for Lydia was now mixed with unspeakable pain. I was filled with grief for my loved one. All the promise of her life as a daughter, a scholar, a friend, a wife, a mother was lying silently in a highly-polished box made of Australian red cedar, lined in rose-pink silk, and fastened tightly with shiny brass screws.

It was a beautiful box, for a beautiful girl, but I was struggling to accept the reality of it holding my daughter from now until forever.

Lydia—it was such an old-fashioned name for one who had died so young. She had been seventeen! Well, seventeen and a bit, but not much more. Like all her friends, Lydia had been more than three-quarters of the way through her last year of high school, only ten days away from sitting for her final exams. Her end-of-year ballgown, wrapped in cellophane to protect it from dust, hung on the hook behind her bedroom door.

Everyone had been in to see it, all of her aunts and our friends around the neighbourhood. Lydia had hunted high and low for just the right dress. It had to be a grown-up dress, but not too grown-up. The dress was a rainbow of colours, and it embodied Lydia's personality to a T. No single, solid colour would have ever expressed who Lydia was. Her life had always been full of fun, and full of colour, and that was what she had wanted her first formal dress to represent.

The dress had been hanging on the far row, in the very last shop we looked in. We had both been tired of looking, and ready to go home. Then at the last moment, Lydia had glimpsed a small section of the skirt, in a very tightly packed rack, and she had been drawn to the back of the shop. The moment she pulled it down and held it to her body, there was never any thought in her mind that it would not fit. The shop assistant, sensing a sale, had cautiously warned that the dress was a 'one off' from the supplier. Lydia had danced into the fitting room and come out with wonder on her face. 'Oh Mum, look, it fits, it's beautiful, I love it. Oh please, Mum, this is the one.' And it was true, the dress could have been made for her; it fit her to perfection.

I could still see her happiness, and almost hear her excitement. And Lydia had been so eager to show everyone, and so impatient for the dance to begin so that she could wear it. But now it would be worn by her forever.

What had happened?

Would they ever really find out?

The car had not been overloaded. There were only the four of them travelling that night. That stretch of road had been straight and smooth. Lydia had been driving. Her friends had all been sleeping, so were unable to tell the police anything. The police said the road surface was in good condition, and the weather had been dry. They thought that perhaps Lydia may have swerved to avoid a cow. So farm fences for miles around had been checked for breaks, but all of them had been standing firm. No one owned up to any stock being loose on the road. Yet there had been burnt rubber on the bitumen, indicating Lydia had braked hard for nearly twenty yards before the car had left the road.

The police had said it was possible the others had survived because of their relaxed condition. But no one really knew why Lydia had left the road that night, or why only she had died.

Looking at the white, wooden casket holding the mortal remains of the baby girl I had given birth to, I could not help but again wonder, *Why had she hit her brakes so hard that she had left rubber on the road surface? Had she fallen asleep, then suddenly woken up? Maybe there had been a kangaroo, a koala, or a wombat on the road.*

The truth was, if there had been an animal on the road it would not have mattered who was driving, because none of the girls would have wanted to hit an animal with the car. The police investigation report put forward a conclusion in time for the Coroner's Court. The report said that it had been a single-vehicle accident, where the car had been travelling within the speed limit, but the cause of the sudden braking, and change of direction, was undetermined.

What they said, what the coroner recorded, had little effect on my reality. The car crashed and my daughter was dead. Lydia had been a popular young girl with her whole future ahead of her, yet here she was dead. I had been told that the shock of the crash had affected the whole town. Until I looked around, at the sound of people filtering in for the service, I had thought very little about other people.

I watched people I knew walk down the aisle of the beautiful church and find a seat. Some nodded and smiled that smile you give to someone who you do not really want to talk to, because you do not know what to say. I was thankful for their distance. I did not blame them for their distance.

My Lydia was no different from her friends. It could have been any of the girls in the car driving home. That night it had been Lydia. And I could imagine them thinking, *Thank God that it is not our child lying there in a box, for it could so easily have been ours and not hers.* I knew with certainty that they would be saying something like, 'There but for the Grace of God goes us.' Why could I be so certain? Well, I knew that was easy to answer, because there had been moments in the past few days when I had thought, *Why my child? Why Lydia and not one of the other young girls?* So I understood their thoughts, and their distance, because I, too, had thought them.

The girls in the car had been part of a representative basketball team, taking part in a weekend competition being held in a neighbouring town. When the competition finished, late in the afternoon, Lydia and her friends had decided to drive home rather than stay an extra night. They all had school the next day, and did not want to drive the seventy kilometres home before school. Other members of the team had made the same decision, and arrived home safely.

It was a small town and, as such, anything that affected the children of the town affected their parents. What affected the parents affected the family and friends. I had seen how the death of three of the football team affected Lydia. They had been 'hooning' around in the basin of the old granite quarry. Three of them in the tray of the four-wheel drive had been thrown when the vehicle tipped over. Two of them were crushed by the rolling utility, and the other hit his head on a large stone. And that had only been six weeks ago.

The whole town had been affected. Since then, the town centre had been extremely quiet after dark, due to a lack of young drivers doing 'lappies' around the main street. Parents of driving teenagers were limiting their children's freedom, and stressing the need to be alert when driving.

Still, I knew the words of parents would forever go in one ear and out the other of teenagers. Why? *Again, a no-brainer when answering this one,* I thought. Children always think that they know everything and are the first to do anything. My Lydia had been a perfect example. Every time I caught her doing something she knew she shouldn't be doing, she would say, 'Mum, how did you know?'

I would give her my eyebrow-lift look and tell her, 'I wasn't born yesterday. I have been there and done that.' Her look of disbelief always amused me.

Thinking about teenagers, who think they are invincible and above the dangers parents talk about, I was again filled with unanswerable questions.

How do we protect them?

How do we keep them safe?

How can we guide them into adulthood?

How can we keep them alive when there are so many choices to make, choices that can take them away?

No longer able to stand by my precious daughter's coffin, I sat in one of the seats reserved for the bereaved, which were in the front row of the church.

In moving from the casket to the pew, I was aware that people who knew Lydia and me were choosing their own places to sit. I knew this was a sign of respect, and I felt ungrateful in wishing they had stayed away, at least for a while longer. I was not yet ready to say goodbye.

I only vaguely heard the softly murmured greetings, and words spoken to give comfort to those still living, being swallowed in the vastness of the building. I was not conscious of time passing so was totally unprepared to hear the notes of a popular song, about walking through a storm, softly floating around the building. Glancing at my watch, I realised I had been standing longer than I had thought. The music I heard was organized and had started on time. The song playing had been one Lydia had loved.

Lydia had first heard the song at a soccer match, with her father in England. She had been overwhelmed to hear forty thousand voices all singing the one song, and had insisted her father teach it to her. Lydia had been eleven when she had discovered her 'football' song was really about holding onto God's hope during the storms in our lives. When the funeral assistant had asked about which song I wanted to be played at her funeral, there was only one I could choose.

Listening to the music I sighed, she was still so real to me. *Maybe if I concentrate really hard, maybe*

I will hear her, hear the joy in her voice as she sang the song to her God, and not just the music playing.

Her love for Jesus, her love for God, and her acceptance of the Holy Spirit living in her was resolute. At some stage during her Sunday school years, Lydia had just known that they were real, and a living presence in her life. Lydia had lived a life full of thankfulness, and gratitude for everything in her life. Her Jesus had come to save her and He was in her every conversation. At some stage of Lydia's conversations, she always told the person she was talking to that they needed 'to know Jesus died for them'. Jesus was her friend and there was nothing Lydia did that she kept from Him.

I admit there were times when I was a little jealous of this particular friend of Lydia's.

Lydia truly believed her purpose was to tell people about the choice they could make, and she did. I remember finding it 'cute' to see my small daughter go around the tables of a café, telling everyone that Jesus loved her, and He loved them too. Later, as a teenager, I had tried to discourage her from approaching strangers by telling her that 'what was cute as a child is an invasion of another person's privacy when you are not invited to speak to them'. Lydia had found a way around that, too, by first asking the people she approached if she could talk to them.

Her song about 'holding on' and 'walking on' swirled around me as I sat in thought on the wooden pew. I thought about the times when I had not been able to stop her from approaching people, so had physically, and mentally, moved away and tried to disown her. *When,* I thought, *when had I stopped wanting to be seen with her? When had I started to be embarrassed by the words my daughter said?* And I remembered it was about the same time that I had become jealous of her friendship with Jesus. Tears filled my eyes; how stupid could I have been to envy something Lydia gave away so freely. She never excluded anyone from the opportunity to know her friend.

Lydia had no fear, or embarrassment, about telling people Jesus loved them and wanted to be their friend. Just like that, she would approach total strangers. Young, old, in-between, it did not matter who they were. Up she would go in the shopping centres, on the sports fields, at school. Only a few weeks ago I had asked her why she did it, and she had simply said, 'Because time is short, Mum, and people have to know they have a choice to make.'

I felt someone sit beside me. I turned to look into the face of my dear friend Jean, and felt comforted because I was not alone in trying to make sense of this day. While Jean sat silently beside me, I became aware of the whispered movement around me as friends filled the church. I looked briefly to my right, and my left, but found the expressions of sympathy around me too much to endure, so I looked straight ahead. In doing so, I looked straight up into the face of Jesus as he hung on the cross.

For the first time that day I thought, *That's it; now I know that I am losing it,* because the church we were in did not have a figure hanging on the cross in the alcove of the nave.

I recalled that this church celebrated the resurrected Christ—focusing on His work on Earth being done—and so only ever had an empty cross, anchored squarely, on the wall of the nave.

Yet now, gazing up at the wooden cross, framed by the church's largest stained-glass window, I clearly saw a figure nailed to its crosspieces.

Not only was the figure hanging there, some ten feet from the floor, what looked like blood was flowing from the wounds in its hands and feet. The 'blood' on its face ran downwards from cuts caused by the thorns embedded in its forehead. On its naked upper torso, above the cloth wrapped around its hips, was an open wound where something had pierced its side.

As I looked in disbelief at the vision before me, reality faded and time seemed to stop as the figure separated itself from the cross and walked towards me. No longer was it a wooden figure, carved to sit in the middle of a wooden cross; no, with each step I could see the reality of a living human being. With each step, the brightness of the blood on his face and body faded. So, too, did the cloth around his hips. By the time he was standing in front of me, he was clothed in a softly flowing, long white robe, belted by a tie of the same fabric at his waist.

I tried to say something—anything would have done—to dispel the dream I thought I must be having, but nothing came. He raised his right hand from his side and pointed to the seat beside me, asking silently to be invited to sit. How could I refuse?

It was beyond me to refuse the kindness, and love, I saw in his eyes, so I nodded yes and turned in my seat in order to face him. Even as I looked at him in disbelief, he looked at me and I heard him say, 'I as a child came from the Father to experience life as you know it. I came to tell you of the Father's love for you, and His need of your love for Him. I came to give you a way to know the Father as you were meant to know Him.

'The Father created the Heavens and Earth. What the Father created was good, and without blemish. The Father created man, and He walked with man, and He talked with man, and it was good. Man was told, *Do not eat fruit from the tree in the middle the garden, for it will bring death.*

'But man was deceived, and by his own free will ate the fruit. Even as he ate, he knew he was sinning, rebelling against the Father's direction. And in doing so he lost the friendship, the trust and freedom he had with the Father.

'The consequence of man's sin was death. But it was death to his innocence, death to his relationship, friendship, with the Father. Eating the fruit opened his eyes to condemnation and deception. Eating the fruit caused man to live a life with sin in it. God cannot abide sin, so while the man had sin in his heart, in his life, he could not live with God. The only way back to the Father is to be sin free. To be washed in the righteousness of God Himself.

'You are of man, and by your own efforts have no way of overcoming sin in your life, and so cannot know the love of the Father as He intended. The price of sin is death of the sinner, or death of an innocent who would stand in place of the sinner.

'I was, am, and always will be innocent and sin free. On the cross I took on the sins of the world; I became your sin. I offered my life in place of yours. I paid the price of your sin because you never could. I died so that you could live, so that you could know the Father

'I did this out of the love of the Father.

'But being from the Father, and of the Father, I am and always will be part of the Father.

'I lived a life as a man, I died as a man, but I rose victorious over all sin for all time, the Son of God.

'Lydia knew this as something I did for her; she chose to accept the gift of my sacrifice, my gift of love and life. Then she chose to live her life wanting to share her understanding with people. Because of this, Lydia has eternal life and resides with the Father today.

'The Father wants you, by your own free will, to choose to accept the gift of His love by acknowledging that I am His Son, and Your only way to Salvation.

'The Father is gracious and merciful, but the Father has a condition to you accepting His gift. That condition is, it has to be accepted before the death of your human body.

'The result of acceptance is eternal life, love and peace in the presence of the Father. The result of non-acceptance is an eternity living in darkness, where the light and love of God does not exist, an eternity where your spirit is tortured for eternity. The Father alone knows the length of your days; the question for you today is, do you know what Lydia knew?'

Even as I stared at the man in front of me, he faded into nothingness, and I, once again, had a clear view of my daughter's casket. Still in a bit of a daze, and trying to reconcile myself with the vision

I had seen and the words I had heard, I was abruptly brought back into my surrounds as a handbag hit me in the back of my head.

'Oh, sorry, I am so sorry,' apologized a woman I recognised as a neighbour of mine as she sat on the pew behind me.

My friend, Jean, leant towards me and asked, 'Are you okay? You look even paler than you were two minutes ago. Is it your head?'

Even while I nodded, and shook my head to ease her concerns, I was silently thinking, *Wow, that is not exactly the most comforting of things that I thought God would say at a time like this.* If anything, I would have thought it would be more like, *My peace is with you,* not, *Life is short, so what are you going to do about it?*

I looked around, realising that the message, although only heard by me, was not just for me. This message was for everyone who had come that day to say goodbye to my daughter, and even more than that, for their family and friends, too. I had been challenged. I could no longer pretend ignorance over the importance of using my free will. To pretend I did not know would mean that I did not choose to receive the gift of the Good News of Jesus Christ.

I wanted to be, one day, where my daughter was. To go there, I needed to know what Lydia knew, and to walk in that knowledge, sharing it wherever I went.

So, making my choice, knowing that it was the most important moment in my life, I rose from my seat and walked over to the wooden casket that held the earthly body of my daughter. I heard the hush that ran through the church, but took no notice of it. I was not concerned with the comments people were making; I had something much more important on my heart, and mind. The minister, waiting to commence the service to be held over my daughter's body, held his hand up to halt the organist's playing. He descended from his place on the pulpit and came to find out what I, the mother of the deceased, wanted. I asked him if I could have a few moments to speak to everyone in the church. He seemed a bit uncertain, but then again I did not know what his previous experience had been with bereaved relatives. I assured him that I was in a fit condition to speak, so he indicated that I could have my moment to speak before the ceremony started.

I suppose I could have waited. I could have included my new message in my farewell to my darling Lydia, but I knew, deep within me, that this message could not wait. For the first time, I understood Lydia's urgent desire to talk to everyone she met.

Lydia had known that time was short. She had known the only thing that mattered was to give people the chance to choose the gift of love and life that was in Jesus. Because she knew, as I had discovered, that once people had heard of the choice they were then responsible to God for their answer.

I do not know whether Lydia ever knew that not all would choose to know the forgiving, loving grace and mercy of God, but she definitely did know that they had to be offered the opportunity.

Lydia spent her life offering everyone she met the opportunity, and now that I knew, I had the opportunity to do the same as Lydia—or not.

I knew that I was not suddenly healed of the pain in my heart. My heart still ached for the loss of my daughter. My grief was still overwhelming, but within that grief I could feel the touch of a friend. I could feel the touch of Lydia's friend, and found that I had the courage to speak of the Good News that was available to everyone, if only they would accept it. I knew that first the people had to hear about it. So I thanked everyone for coming to share their love and support me. I knew the choice I was making—to tell people what Lydia knew—was the right one for me.

The Hidden Valley

He heard them outside his valley. Listening intently, he could hear living branches screaming for mercy as they were torn from their life force. After each rejected cry, he felt the 'thud' through his roots as they fell heavily to the ground. His grief grew with each agonizing death he heard.

The destruction of whole species of living trees had been going on for so long that he had almost forgotten a time without the cries, and smell, of death weighing in the air around him.

How long before they entered his valley?

How long would it be before they spotted him?

How long would it be before they attacked his lovely limbs, took him apart, carted him away, or left him to rot undetected on the forest floor?

His memory, like that in all of his kind, was long and strong.

He remembered long, long ago, the first autumn of his birth had been long and cold. He had not fallen far from his mother. He could still remember hearing the old ones whisper, high over his head, about the white covering that was coming. *Soon, it will come soon,* some said.

How can you tell? he had queried in his small new voice.

The warmth of the autumn sun is weakening. The daylight hours are shorter, his mother whispered, in an effort to distract her son from disturbing the talk of the elders.

Every tree he could hear agreed the season was changing. Soon the talk turned to guessing how long the cold would stay, and what effect it would have on their growth rings. Within days of feeling a chill about his soil, he had tasted the promise of the 'white covering'. It had come on the wind, as it rushed through his valley blowing down from the high peaks of the mountains.

His mother had protected him through his first winters. She had accepted the 'white covering' he came to know as snow, allowed it to settle on her limbs so that its weight helped to keep her lowest branches around her little seedling. She took the worst of it from him, but even so he had been soon covered by the whiteness, and he had slept his first winters cocooned within the snow.

He had been in his seventh ring growth when he thought his trunk was strong enough to withstand the harsh winter winds and heavy snowfalls without his mother's protection. His roots had sunk deep into the soil, and were holding him firm. He rejoiced, his mother and the trees around him rejoiced; he had survived his seedling years. Now he could look forward to being part of the forest for years to come.

In his tenth ring growth, disaster came to his valley. That year, the rain, normally a welcome friend, had shown the young tree just how powerful it could be. The thunder that came before it had tried to warn every living thing—vegetable, mineral and animal—but no one could have foretold the extent of the damage, misery and pain to come. The young tree had never known anything like it. The rain was so heavy for days that the little tree had to grab hard to the soil in order to stop his roots from being exposed to the weather. Then the rain had stopped, but the danger had not gone away. Only days after the sun showed its face to the young tree, the ground under his mother had just slipped away. And she fell, roots and all. With her went several of the older trees closer to the ravine. One moment he had been standing in her shadow, and then he was alone. Hearing her die the long slow death of the dislodged could have been terrible, but her love for her little sapling had her fighting against the pain of starvation, and talking to him about the wonderful life he would have.

She told him he was from a large family who grew tall, straight and strong all over both sides of the high mountain ranges. The young tree listened to his mother while she told him that all living things would stop and listen when the wind blew. She told him the wind was their friend. Without the wind, the trees would not be warned in advance of danger. Without the wind, they would not receive news from faraway old friends and family. Then one day she stopped talking, and started her journey into the next part of her purpose for living. The young tree knew it had to happen this way, but for many ring growths he had been sad.

Over the years he remembered his mother's love of the wind, especially when the wind carried a tang of salt to leave on his leaves. The wind left not only the smell and taste of the lands over the mountains, but also mental pictures of where it had been, and what it had seen. The tree gathered his mother's love of the wind and added to it his own. He was always happy to hear the wind tell how it raced with the water as it built into peaks of white foam. The wind was with the waves until their race ended, as they thumped onto the rocks at the feet of the mountains. That was when the wind would snatch at the salty drops of water, and carry them high up and over the mountain peaks.

The now maturing tree enlarged his pictures with every word the wind whispered on its way through the valley. The wind told its listeners how the rocks never spoke, but were seriously, solidly committed to their task of protecting the land. 'Their job is to repel the salty, poisonous ocean waves from reaching the living trees and shrubs of the land.'

During his years as a sapling, the tree had not understood how something so dangerous to his kind could possibly be good for something else. The wind insisted 'furry animals swam in the salty water and birds with webbed feet rode the waves, diving under them to catch their food. At times the furry animals and the birds would both come out of the water settle onto the rocks to rest before going back into the water.'

The seasons were good to the young tree, and he grew strong, straight and tall. One day he heard the wind bring word of dark-skinned creatures that moved around the land on two legs; these creatures were known to the older trees at the foot of the valley. 'We used to see these creatures moving down by the river's edge. They never stayed long, but they are known to us.'

The wind, not to be outdone in the information department, whispered on its way, 'But did you know that the two-legged creatures hunted the furry little animals when they came to rest on the rocks?'

Sometimes the wind would carry a hint of smoke from their fires. Another time the wind talked of wooden things, with billowing sheets of white clouds, racing with the wind across the salty water. The wind told of other two-legged creatures, like the ones who hunted the furry animals, but these were pale in colour.

The wind had nearly snorted its superiority when it told of the wooden thing running directly into the rock, as though it were an ocean wave. As it broke apart and sank into the salty water the pale, two-legged creatures had come hurrying out of the belly of the wooden thing. This news, like so much of the news brought by the wind, was heard with interest but given little thought by the trees of the valley. After all, what happened on the far side of the mountains rarely affected the valley. So he, like all of his kind in the valley, forgot about the plight of the creatures that had been washed out of the belly of the broken wooden thing.

The tall, strong tree knew from his seasons in the valley that there were times when every living thing across the land paid great attention to messages in the wind. When the wind whispered danger, all ears heard. Danger existed in various forms for the trees and creatures of the land. Creatures were in danger from other creatures, and the dark two-legged animal that killed with stone and stick. Trees along the riverbanks dug their roots in deep when the rains filled the river and turned it into a raging torrent of destructive power. The one thing that brought fear into every heart was the whispered word of fire. When the heavens roared and shot spears of light to the ground, dry, withered, discarded leaves were struck and became a thing feared by every living thing. Fire had no compassion, no mercy. Fire, once started, raced, jumped, exploded and burnt for as long, and as far, as it could go.

Word of fire was a two-edged sword to the trees of the land. Even though fire germinated the next generation of seedlings, it was still a thing to be feared, because fire also destroyed. When the temperature of a racing fire was too hot, the life-sap of a tree exploded. When the fire moved slowly through the forest, it took hold of a tree's core and ate away at it until there was nothing left but a blackened empty shell.

Then, one day, the wind had carried a different sound, a sound so sad that all movement around the tall tree stopped. He remembered that day as though it had just happened.

The sound had come with the wind, but after the wind had gone there had been stillness in the air. The tall, strong tree had never felt anything like it. It was as though the very air itself was holding its breath, waiting to be told what to do next. Slowly, almost hesitantly, the air around him had shifted, and things around the tree seemed to return to normal.

A light breeze, one that only ever came to play, danced through the leaves of his branches. Trees around him returned to talking about the sun, the moon, anything, in an effort to deny the sounds they had heard in the wind. But he knew, as the others did, that he had not imagined the sound; it had been the sound of great death. Sadness settled in his heart and he grieved for lost lives.

He was a Great Red Cedar, and he had come from a long line of Great Red Cedars. He counted his time on Earth in the number of growth rings inside his large, strong, straight trunk. He had already lived for more than four hundred rings when the sound came, and his land changed.

Even though no one wanted to hear of the devastation happening on the other side of the mountains, the wind continued to bring news to the valley. The wind told of the decimation of the felled trees, stripped of their beautiful limbs and dragged to the water's edge then towed away by ships throwing out foul-smelling fumes.

The wind was no longer filled with the sweet scent of pine, eucalyptus, blossom or salt. It was smoke heavy, and hard on the leaves of all trees. There was nothing in the wind but the unfamiliar noises of things that killed. Everyone in his valley had become silent as they grieved for lost friends. All living things knew there was One who was able to save them. During the life span of most trees and creatures of the land, they had never had a need to call on the One who could. The One they all knew to be the Creator of all things. But from the time of 'the sound', many called on the Creator, asking for the safety of their valley, and their lives.

Many seasons passed; he heard older trees making the sweetness of the wind folklore. A story, based on truth, to tell the seedlings, in the hope all who had perished would be remembered. Because in the story was all the good news the wind used to carry: the tang of salt, furry creatures who swam in the salty water and sat on the rocks, and how healthy and happy everything on the other side of the mountains used to be.

Then came a day more dreadful than any other: one day the destructive things appeared on his side of the mountains. He had thought nothing could be worse than the sounds and smells carried on the wind. But now the wind was not the messenger. Now he could see, smell and hear them for himself. And a more ominous sound than that of the dull thud of something cutting into solid tree trunk he could never have imagined. The sound was always accompanied by the cries and desolate screams of those who were dying, one thud at a time. Then the haze of wood smoke sent up from the many trees burning on the sides of the mountains filled the horizon. Day and night, he could see the red flicker of fire.

Day and night, the killing things made their awful noise. Day and night, they inched closer and closer to his valley.

From his place high up in his valley, he could see the stripped mountain ranges. He had grown tall seeing only green treetops and blue sky, but now he could see the brown cleared land, and he feared for the life of his valley.

More time passed before he saw the animals that lived on the ground of his valley begin to hide during the daylight hours. Something had them running for cover to hide in the shadows of his branches. Hiding from noises they did not recognise. Then one day he saw a new thing. From his position in the valley, he saw a different creature. It did not tread softly through the undergrowth of the forest. It did not run for cover out of a fear of being seen, but travelled in groups making lots of noise.

These new pale-skinned, two-legged creatures travelled with carts made of wood he did not recognise; the carts were pulled by four-legged animals with horns. Watching the heavyset animals shove their way through the young brush tore at his heart. They appeared to have no concern about the damage they were doing. The carts they pulled could not sidestep or twist around a young sapling; they were fixed and rigid. If they had only been wheels, then perhaps the young saplings might have been able to spring back, and survive. But from his vantage point high up the valley, the tall tree saw the wooden crates between the wheels catch hold of, then tear, the saplings out by their roots, leaving them to die.

Even as the Great Red Cedar grieved for the loss of young lives, he discovered the real danger to the forest was not from the carts pulled by the great horned beasts, but from the pale, two-legged creatures. It was only when more upright creatures joined the first ones, holding unfamiliar things from their carts and swinging them towards the bases of mature trees that the Great Red Cedar's heart shattered. He heard the dull 'thud' 'thud' 'thud', then, as trees under attack cried out for mercy, he realised that the enemy of his kind had arrived.

From his vantage point at the top end of his valley, he watched helplessly as the trees outside his valley were chopped down and carted away. Worst of all were the death cries of the juvenile trees, which had barely passed their tenth ring. He wept at the waste, as they were cut just inches from the ground, to be the railings of square areas used to contain the four-legged animals at night. They were used for only a moment in time, then forgotten, left to slowly disintegrate. He wept for their loss. He wept hot sap from every part of his trunk for the loss of the ring growths they would never know, for the conversations they could no longer join.

And still they came—those pale, two-legged creatures who called themselves men, to cut down and destroy the tree-covered mountains and valleys growing back from the sea. Soon the wind carried poisoned air that poured from their factories. The foul air settled on the topmost branches of the eldest, and tallest, members of his kind in the valley.

The pale, two-legged creatures did not ever come into his valley. Even though he, and the others with him, waited to accept the inevitable, the pale creatures never came. He saw them when the wind blew away the cloud of foul air that covered the land outside his valley. Many times he had held his leaves still, kept them silent, when the two-legged creatures hunted and killed close to the entrance of his valley. But they never came. It was as though his valley had been hidden from their sight, protected by an unseen hand.

As the seasons passed, he watched the 'old ones' near the entrance of the valley stretch out their limbs trying to protect the young saplings, and give them time to grow. They reached out, trying to take the worst of the foul air, trying to filter it in the hope of giving the younger trees time to gain the strength to survive this attack from the air. But in doing so they they took the foul air deep within, but could not process it. The build-up of poisoned air was too much for their life force; they could not rid themselves of it, so before his eyes they slowly withered and died themselves.

Many more seasons passed and, silently, sorrowfully, he watched the land surrounding the river outside his valley cleared of living trees. Even when there were no more trees to cut down and take away, more of the two-legged creatures came to his land. The two-legged creatures he had heard the furry, hopping animals that hoped under his branches call men no longer travelled with carts pulled by horned animals, but came in big, and little, things that seemed to move faster than the wind.

He watched as the violated area around the river was re-covered with square and rectangular boxes. With much unnatural noise, the number of boxes grew daily, clustering together to cover both sides of the river's banks. Noisy machines used to build the boxes carried their own foul smell and added to the smell of death.

The Great Red Cedar saw the men go into the belly of the boxes at night, then come out when the sun rose in the morning. There were many things the Great Red Cedar did not understand; one of them was how the pale, two-legged creatures survived spending the night inside the boxes that screamed death, but they did. Another was how his valley had remained undiscovered by men. Both were things he accepted as being unknown to him, and so philosophically he set his mind to carry on with the order of his life until he could not. Such was the way of nature.

More seasons passed and still his valley remained undiscovered from the men. Being well into his seven-hundredth growth ring, he was the oldest of his kind still living in the valley. He had taken on the role of teaching the younger trees the history of the land. He often talked of the old days, telling the younger ones how the wind had carried the tang of salt, and news of friends. However, the saplings around him had never known this news-carrying wind, so he hoped they believed he told the truth, and did not speak only to encourage them to survive.

Then, one day, while the sun shone with its usual brilliance, he heard another softer, hesitant noise. He waited. Something within was both terrified and expectant. From his towering height at the head of the valley, he saw something that held his interest. It was a small movement, a flash of brown; something—some creature—was wandering slowly, quietly, almost gently, amongst the trees at the mouth of his valley. It looked like one of the men, not in a shiny thing that moved too fast to be seen, but on the back of a four-legged animal the tree had heard the furry, hopping creatures call horse.

He had often seen these four-legged animals— *horse,* he reminded himself—running in herds beneath his branches and through his valley. The strange thing was, he had never before seen a man on the back of a horse. When horses ran beneath him they had always seemed to be in a hurry to get back into the mountains, and away from the man. This horse, however, seemed to be very accepting of the man on his back. So the Great Red Cedar watched and waited.

He could not move, because he was rooted deep into the earth, so he silently watched the man on the horse travel from tree trunk to tree trunk. Carefully he skirted around granite boulders that were randomly scattered throughout the valley floor. From the tree's vantage point, he saw how the placement of the boulders made it difficult for men to see a way into the valley. However, it appeared to the tree that this man was not to be stopped. He took his time reaching the bottom of the ravine at the head of the valley. It was from the heights of this ravine that the Great Red Cedar had watched the world outside his valley change. So, when the man and horse found a way to climb up the sides of the ravine, and reached the Great Red Cedar, he felt fear flitter throughout his leaves.

For the longest time nothing happened. Then the man got down from the horse and stood looking up into the Great Red Cedar's tallest branches. The man stretched back his head, lifting a hand to shade his eyes from the sunlight as he peered into the highest branches of the tree, a tree that should not have survived the long years of logging.

The beautiful, seven-hundred-year-old Great Red Cedar stood taller than he had ever stood before. Something inside pressed him to know this moment was important, not just for him but for his entire valley. The wind, that had brought no good news for many season suddenly whispered, 'This is your time to shine. It was for this time you were grown, from seed to the tree you are. Stand tall, reach for the Heavens above. Be proud of who you are.'

The voice of the wind gave him strength to overcome his fear of the men, and he stretched as far, and as wide, as he was able. He moved his upper branches in time with the wind whispering around him, and let the man see him in all his glory. He was nearly the last of his kind and he knew it. The wind had told him all but a hidden few were gone.

The man hesitantly walked forward, reached out a hand, and, touching the Great Red Cedar's magnificent trunk, whispered words that the tree could not understand. The man walked all the way around the base of the tree, looked down the ravine, took some strange things out of the side of the horse, measured the tree's girth, tested the soil between the tree's roots, talked into his hand, then, after a long time, the man took the horse back down the ravine.

After again looking up the height of the ravine, the man jumped onto the horse's back and rode down the valley and was gone from sight.

The Great Red Cedar watched the man go; just as the tree had watched the horse carefully walk through his valley he watched it leave.

The Great Red Cedar was unsure of his feelings. It was the first time he had seen one of the pale, two-legged creatures that the furry hopping creatures called men. From his experience of watching men from a distance, the tree knew this meeting with a man could mean the end of him, and his valley. The Great Red Cedar did not know what would happen, now that men had discovered a way into his valley. He hoped the 'unseen presence' that had kept his valley hidden and safe from destruction would continue to protect them all.

He had done all that he could to survive in the changing times. Like the older ones at the beginning of the foul air, he had helped those around him. He had taught the younger ones how to limit the amount of foul air they breathed in, until each of them found a way to breathe and survive on their own. He had encouraged hope with stories of the wind and time of sweet air. He had mourned the loss of the old ones when they had no longer been able to process the foul-smelling air, and fallen to the forest floor.

He was long lasting, he was a survivor, but he could not stop wondering whether the man's presence in his valley was a warning that it was soon to be his time to go.

He had survived because he had been stoically patient. So he did what he did best. He waited, and he waited, but nothing happened. Summer came and went, autumn winds blew, and the white covering came with the winter. Then the softer winds of spring came again, yet still nothing happened. Another round of seasons came and went, and still another, and another. Time passed. The Great Red Cedar was beginning to think that perhaps nothing would ever happen, and then he saw them.

More of them were coming. All on the backs of the animals they called horses. At first he had heard them loudly talking, and laughing, until they entered the outer rim of his valley. Then there had been silence. The silence from the men had radiated up the valley, up the ravine, past the Great Red Cedar, and kept on going. Everything within the valley remained paused in response to the silence. The Great Red Cedar watched as some of the men slowly and carefully approached some of the younger trees. They, too, pulled things out of the middle of the horses and touched the bark of the trees. The Great Red Cedar felt for them, those young ones who were only now reaching their one- and two-hundredth rings of growth; he hoped the men would touch them as gently as the first man had touched his trunk. He did not know what would happen, but he desperately wanted the younger trees to retain a good memory of men. He felt this was important.

The Great Red Cedar had no idea that these men, creatures, had worked hard to save him, and his hidden valley. He had no idea they were astounded because the God they believed in had planted, grown, and protected him during one of man's most destructive times. A time when men had almost succeeded in ridding the world of wonders like him. He did not know that because of the battle of words of one man, all living things in this valley would survive to live out their natural lives in peace, without risk of destruction.

The Great Red Cedar did not know that because of him, because he had survived and encouraged others to survive, this place, his valley, was being protected as a place of peace and wonder. The man on his horse had known immediately how amazing the valley was, as soon as he had wandered into it. The man had petitioned his government for man's protection to be placed over the valley. He had concluded his petition with a piece of his own wonder. 'I can only put forward my reason for this valley's survival as being one of divine intervention. For surely the natural growth in this valley could only have escaped obliteration because it has been hidden in plain sight for so many years, by a power greater than the destruction of man.'

The man knew people would come, as soon as he saw it, he had known and he had gone to the government. It had been a long, hard fight, but he knew it was right to turn the whole valley into a national park. The name he had given it was Godspeed National Park. For nowhere else in the world had he stood beneath strong, healthy, towering trees designed to turn poisoned air into something sweet and pure. The man had known, deep in his heart, that the valley was a place where people could see, and feel, God at work.

The man hoped people would see how God had reached out his hand to protect this valley, and these trees. When the rest of the land around them was in turmoil and being destroyed, God had looked and said, 'Enough. This I will save from the destruction of man.'

The man hoped that after spending time in the protected park people would know that God was aware of the trouble that surrounded the valley. God loved this valley. And God protected, and provided, all that was needed for the valley to survive. In the face of certain destruction, God had delivered salvation. He hoped the people who visited the valley would go back to their own worlds, believing that God could, and would, do the same for them.

The Cat Loved Water

T'was the night before Christmas,
When all through the house,
Not a creature was stirring,
Not even a mouse.

The time for thinking and planning was over. There was no more time, and there were no more plans to be made.

It was Christmas Eve. The children were tucked up in their beds already asleep. The dog had been out for an evening walk, and the cat was dead. And that was certainly not the way I intended the day to finish, with the cat limping home to die on the front step.

There were many ways that I would have preferred a big day out to end, but finding a loved pet dead on the front doorstep was certainly not on the top of my list. The cat had been missing for the nearly a week. We had placed a lost-and-found advertisement in the local paper and had it read over the radio's local community announcements. But nothing had come from them.

The children insisted we take a picture of the cat to the local animal pound. We had wanted to ensure she would be recognised as soon as she was brought in. With their kind assurances that they would ring us if the cat turned up at the pound, I had dragged the children away. All the while encouraging them to believe the cat would be returned to their little arms. But, being a realist at heart, after the fifth day I doubted we would ever see the cat again. As the wage earner of the household, I had not been too upset about the cat's disappearance, especially when I thought about saving on the cost of good-quality kitty litter. Still, I would not have wanted the cat dead.

And especially not dead in front of the children!

Trying to pacify the children by telling them that the cat was in a better place had not helped, because they thought that this home—their home—was the best place of all. Telling them that God must have wanted our cat as His own pet had not helped either, because they figured that He, being God, could have had His pick of all the cats in the world ... so why did He have to want theirs?

I made cups of hot chocolate in the hope that, with mouths full, they would listen while I explained to them that God has a plan for everyone, and everything, on Earth—even their little cat. It worked. Soon they were talking about all the good things that had happened to them since the cat had come to live with us.

The cat had just turned up one rainy night. There she was, sitting on the front doorstep all wet and bedraggled. I had often thought that cats had better sense than to sit in the rain, but this cat never was the same as other cats I had known. The children had, of course, been over the moon. They had been at me for ages to get a cat, but I always put them off because we already had a dog as our family pet.

So this gift from thin air was an answer to their hopeful prayers. They welcomed the newcomer into our household as though we were being visited by royalty. And, of course, from the very first lap of milk and cuddle in an old towel, the cat had taken over the household.

I have to admit that the consequences of our extended family were more beneficial than I could have expected. For me, I know that if it had not been for the cat I would not now be such great friends with Mrs Knight. Mrs Knight had already been living in the house next door when we moved in. And, even though I had often taken the high road when I chided the children for calling her 'Old Grumpy', I had been less than kind in my own comments when she complained about their loud voices.

Mrs Knight had always grumbled that the children made too much noise in the backyard, especially when they played with the hose on those hot summer afternoons. She had been most upset to see the children cuddling the cat, and running through the stream of water from the hose. She had yelled at them to stop. So they had stopped, dropped the cat, and to the surprise of Mrs Knight, the cat had then walked to the hose and sat down in front of the stream of water pouring onto the grass.

That was a talking point, and it had given us all the opportunity to get to know each other. Now the children went to Mrs Knight's after school each day for freshly cooked cake and milk. The relief I felt, the weight that had been lifted from my shoulders, knowing that I had found a reliable babysitter, had brought a new lightness to my day, and allowed me to believe we would, as a family, be okay.

It seems so silly now, but less than a year ago my mornings had started with my first waking moments filled with worrying about what the next disaster would be. I dreaded even getting out of bed. At that time, I could see no way of our future ever changing. Less than a year ago, that first step out of bed each morning had been such an effort.

Last Christmas day had come and gone, and the mere thought of entering the new year the same way I had left the old one—struggling to bring up the children and hold down full-time work—had been more than I could bear to think about. Planning for a 'happy new year' had certainly been nothing that I wanted to do. Then the Heavens had opened, and the cat had turned up on our doorstep, and with her, hope came in; and not only for me.

I had not known Mrs Knight had been an active Christian before her husband died. I had no way of knowing that she blamed God for taking her beloved Joe and leaving her alone.

I did not know she blamed God so much she had stopped going to church. She had stopped interacting with people, not only from her church but from her neighbourhood as well. Unknown to me, Mrs Knight's heartache had stopped her wanting to be with anyone. Then, one day, she had looked over the fence and shouted at the children, and found herself opening up to the world again. All because of a cat, a cat that was different.

Mrs Knight later told me that it seemed as though suddenly she was running into the people from her church; and she was once again chatting with the neighbours while she shopped.

Suddenly, she was smiling again and looking forward to each day.

Suddenly, she was letting God reach in to soften her heart toward Him.

Suddenly, her renewed joy in life was too much for her to contain, and so, soon after the episode with the cat and the hose, Mrs Knight cooked a cake and asked me over for a cup of tea. She said she wanted to apologise for her bad attitude. Soon we were talking, laughing and crying as we shared our stories. I found I was able to talk about my concerns of being a single mum, and Mrs Knight shared her fears of never being needed again.

And we found that problems shared could become problems solved.

Over the next few months, Mrs Knight talked about a friend I never knew I had; I remember how I had not wanted to accept I could be loved just because I was me.

I believed no one got anything for nothing, so in all my love relationships I had been a worker, a peacemaker, but nothing I did had ever been enough to keep the men I loved from walking out on me. In the end I had accepted that no one could ever love me enough to want to stay with me.

So how could I now, suddenly, believe I was enough for this friend of Mrs Knight's?

Mrs Knight talked about how God the Father created the Heavens and the Earth. She talked about how He, God, had created people and how, over time, they had turned away from living God's way.

Mrs Knight told me about the Father, and how He had sent His Son to tell the people about the love He had for them. I cried when she told me how some of the people turned against the Son and sent Him to die on the cross.

But then, amazingly, Mrs Knight had said, 'Don't be sad for the Son, be sad for the people. He, the Son, knew He would die a horrible death even before He came live as a man.'

I was stunned to hear this and asked, 'But why, why would the Son still come if He knew He would die like that?'

Mrs Knight had gently smiled and said, 'People sin, and sin is hateful to God. God loved the person who sinned, but He hated sin itself. And anyone who lives with sin has to live without knowing God's love. The price for forgiveness of sin is death. Sin had to be covered in the lifeblood of an innocent. Before the Son came to Earth, people would offer up the innocent lives of animals in exchange for God's forgiveness. But God knew there was a better way, and that was if the people paid for the sin themselves. God, however, loved his people and did not want them to actually die, so God sent His Son to pay the price of sin.

'The Son knew that for the people to be forgiven of all their sin, He, the Son would have to pay the price for them. He would die in their place and He would give to them God's forgiveness, because His blood was shed instead of theirs. This we know as "the Good News" because the Son, Jesus, gave us a way to be forgiven and forever able to know God's love, individually. To receive forgiveness, people need to accept, and believe, that Jesus is the Son of God, and He died so that they would not have to.'

To make sure that I understood her meaning, Mrs Knight then pointedly said, 'The Son, Jesus Christ, took my place and died for my sins. He died for your sins.'

I remember denying that I sinned. Mrs Knight's eyes had softened with understanding before explaining, 'A sin against God can be as simple as a white lie, or as huge as murdering someone. No one on this Earth is without sin.' And I knew it was true.

Deep in my heart I hungered for this forgiveness and love. But I did not really believe that it was for me. I was torn in two because my heart I cried out for it.

Then one day Mrs Knight said something that opened a door into my lonely heart. She said, 'It is easy to believe that Jesus came for the whole world, but it is not until we bring the message found in the Bible down to a personal level, see it as a love letter to us, that we have even the smallest chance of understanding how our separation from Father God is breaking His heart.'

I remember saying, 'I am sorry, I don't understand.'

Mrs Knight had patted my hand and, with great patience, replied, 'While the Bible message is about the whole world, it is also about the individual. If you were the only person on Earth, the Son, Jesus Christ, would still have come. Because not only does God love us all, He sees us all. He does not compare us with each other. He does not hold our past mistakes against us. He is not surprised by us. And He accepts us all, just as we are, because He made us to be who we are.

'He made you, He sees you and He loves you. And because God loves you, so does Jesus. That is why He came. He came so that you would know that, to Him, you were worth dying for. It is the Son's gift to you, and His gift to Father God, and it is free. You do not have to do a single thing but accept His gift.'

Finally I got it!

I finally heard I was enough for Him. He knew everything about me; He saw me warts and all, and He still loved me. Then I had the most wonderful thought flow through me: if I could accept the truth of what I heard, if I could let Jesus into my life, I need never be alone again.

That life-changing revelation, only a few months old, is particularly precious to me on this Christmas Eve, and then I found my thoughts turning to conception, and childbirth. *Odd* I thought, *but then why is it odd? My children, and God's child, needed both to be born. So it really is not so strange to be thinking of such things, because I am, after all, here waiting until my own children have settled for the night. And so, by extension, it is natural that I should be thinking about children … childbirth … my own and another one, who came as a baby to grow into a man destined to die, to pay a debt that was not His.*

I cannot help but be amazed, all over again, every time I remember the miracle of Jesus, the Son who came. He was with God in the beginning of time. He is part of the power of creation that is our God. He chose to separate Himself from God, chose to learn what is like to live as a man, and chose to accept the role of sacrificial lamb for the sins all mankind commits. He, like mankind, had a choice to make. Because He was Jesus, the Son of God, He could have, at any time during His time on Earth, asked God to spare Him the pain of the cross. But, out of love for God the Father, and love for mankind, He chose to come. He chose to stay the distance.

What then, what about the woman-child who bore Him? We call her the Mother of Christ. But the reality is that at the time of conception she was just a young girl who gave birth to a child, as many young girls have done. She nursed her baby, changed his clothes, and taught him his lessons. She would have seen him playing with the other village children and worked beside her husband. She would have loved him with her whole heart, not just because he was God's child, but because he was her baby. Would she have changed anything if she knew that, centuries after her child was born, she would be regarded with love by people all over the world? I don't think she would have done anything differently, because she was a mum with a bub.

The Bible tells me that Mary had loved her God so much so that when sent His angel to ask her to carry a child for Him, she said yes. I believe that because God made us all with free will Mary also had a choice. I do not know whether she gave any thought to her circumstances, or what her family would think, but I do know she chose to accept the task she was being given.

Mary lived in a time where having a child out of marriage was a very bad thing. However, my understanding of the retelling of her story in the Bible says she replied willingly. In faith, it says, Mary surrendered her life, and her body, over to God without asking the consequences.

I do not know how long the conversation was. I am just extremely glad that her answer was, 'Yes, Lord. Let Your Will be done in me.' Because when this young girl trusted in a God who loved her, Jesus came.

As I sat thinking on how God had worked in Mary's life, I realised that when I had comforted my children by telling them, 'God has a plan for everyone and everything,' I had been talking about my own life as well. It suddenly seemed so clear— without my busy job, without my children, without the cat, without Mrs Knight, I would not now be sitting in my kitchen ready to retire for the night with peace in my heart. Seeing a glimpse of God's plan working for me, working for my family, working for Mrs Knight, I whispered, 'Thank you, Jesus. Thank you, God, for showing me I am not alone.'

Rising from my chair, intending to lock up for the night, I paused and again heard the words of the nursery rhyme as they rose up in my mind:

T'was the night before Christmas
When all through the house,

... only to discover they were replaced with words coming through the presence of God's Holy Spirit in my heart, reminding me that the true reason for the Christmas season's celebrations was because over two thousand years ago a babe was born in Bethlehem.

Then the angel said to them, 'Do not be afraid, for behold, I bring you good tidings of great joy ... For there is born to you this day in the city of David a Saviour who is Christ the Lord,' and with the angel appeared a multitude of the Heavenly host praising God, and saying, 'Glory to God in the highest, And on Earth, peace, goodwill toward men!'

Without warning, splitting the silence of night, church bells joyously rang out, loudly announcing the beginning of Christmas Day. As I turned to switch off the downstairs lights, I smiled and knew I was happy to trust in God's promise that there will, one day, be peace on Earth and goodwill in the hearts of all men.

About the Author

Suzanne's characters are written into stories that are the culmination of life events, and moral teachings; God breathed excitement and a desire to share from her experiences and imagination.

Suzanne, a loving daughter, mother and grandmother, is passionate about using stories to impart life lessons in a loving and gentle way, as in the parables of old.

Suzanne remembers her younger years visiting her grandparents' small property as being foundationally important to her. It was through these times that Suzanne developed her ability to 'hear' and 'see' personalities in the things around her. During her time in the country Suzanne gathered an understanding of 'looking out for one's neighbours' and trusting God to provide for the land. Suzanne's parents modelled the value of hard work, while providing a safe home environment filled with love, support, encouragement.

Suzanne believes life is filled with choices all carrying a certain amount of risk. Some of that risk can be seen and accepted before making the choice. Some risk however is either unclear or hidden at the time of making the choice, and often brings pain and disillusionment when uncovered. Suzanne writes to encourage people who are in pain to know that the healer of all pain is waiting to help them.

Suzanne's stories are delivered in easy to read, understandable language. Stories she is hoping you will enjoy and want to share with others.